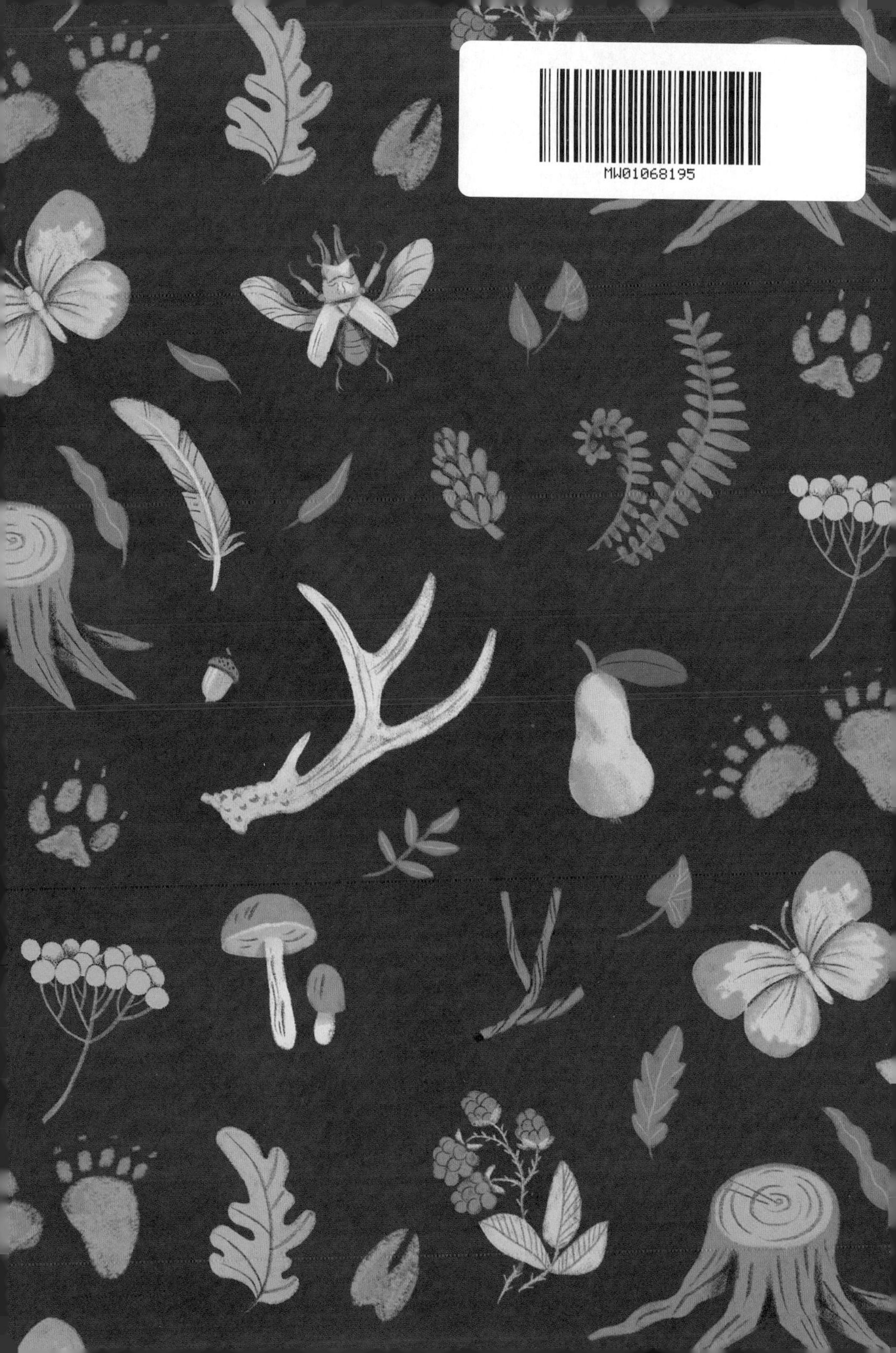

THIS BOOK BELONGS TO:

_____

HOW TO SPOT A MAGICAL WOODLAND CREATURE

HOW TO SPOT A MAGICAL WOODLAND CREATURE

A FIELD GUIDE TO ENCHANTED FOREST ANIMALS

SARAH GLENN MARSH

Illustrated by **LILLA BÖLECZ**

RP|KIDS

PHILADELPHIA

Text copyright © 2025 by Sarah Glenn Marsh
Interior and cover illustrations copyright © 2025 by Lilla Bölecz
Cover copyright © 2025 by Hachette Book Group, Inc.

Hachette Book Group supports the right to free expression and the value of copyright.
The purpose of copyright is to encourage writers and artists
to produce the creative works that enrich our culture.

The scanning, uploading, and distribution of this book without permission is a theft
of the author's intellectual property. If you would like permission to use material from
the book (other than for review purposes), please contact permissions@hbgusa.com.
Thank you for your support of the author's rights.

Running Press Kids
Hachette Book Group
1290 Avenue of the Americas, New York, NY 10104
www.runningpress.com/rpkids
@runningpresskids

First Edition: April 2025

Published by Running Press Kids, an imprint of Hachette Book Group, Inc.
The Running Press Kids name and logo are trademarks of Hachette Book Group, Inc.

The Hachette Speakers Bureau provides a wide range of authors for speaking
events. To find out more, go to www.hachettespeakersbureau.com
or email HachetteSpeakers@hbgusa.com.

Running Press books may be purchased in bulk for business, educational,
or promotional use. For more information, please contact your local bookseller or the
Hachette Book Group Special Markets Department at Special.Markets@hbgusa.com.

The publisher is not responsible for websites (or their content)
that are not owned by the publisher.

Print book cover and interior design by Sara Puppala

Library of Congress Cataloging-in-Publication Data
Names: Marsh, Sarah Glenn, author. | Bölecz, Lilla, illustrator.
Title: How to spot a magical woodland creature : a field guide to enchanted forest animals /
Sarah Glenn Marsh ; illustrated by Lilla Bölecz.
Description: First edition. | Philadelphia : RP Kids, 2025. |
Audience: Ages 8-12 | Audience: Grades 2-3
Identifiers: LCCN 2024025760 (print) | LCCN 2024025761 (ebook) |
ISBN 9780762488049 (hardcover) | ISBN 9780762488056 (ebook)
Subjects: LCSH: Animals, Mythical—Juvenile literature. |
Forest animals—Juvenile literature.
Classification: LCC GR825 .M214 2025 (print) |
LCC GR825 (ebook) | DDC 398.24/54—dc23/eng/20240702
LC record available at https://lccn.loc.gov/2024025760
LC ebook record available at https://lccn.loc.gov/2024025761

ISBNs: 978-0-7624-8804-9 (hardcover), 978-0-7624-8805-6 (ebook)

Printed in Guangdong, China

1010

10 9 8 7 6 5 4 3 2 1

For Lady, Romeo,
Juliet, Khaleesi, Grimm,
Gatsby, Guinness, Bat,
and Dutchess, who
showed me the magic
in being wild at heart.

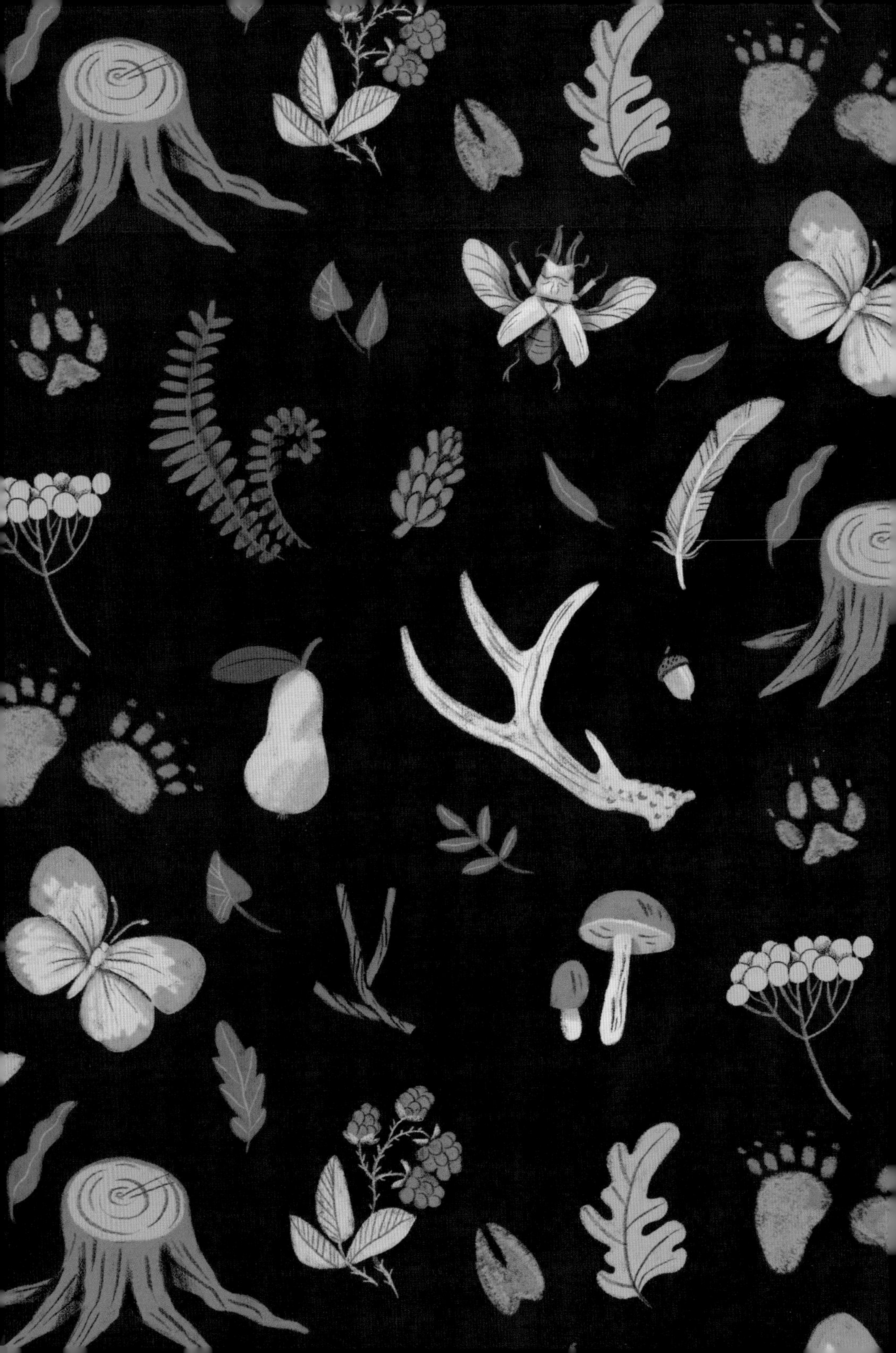

CONTENTS

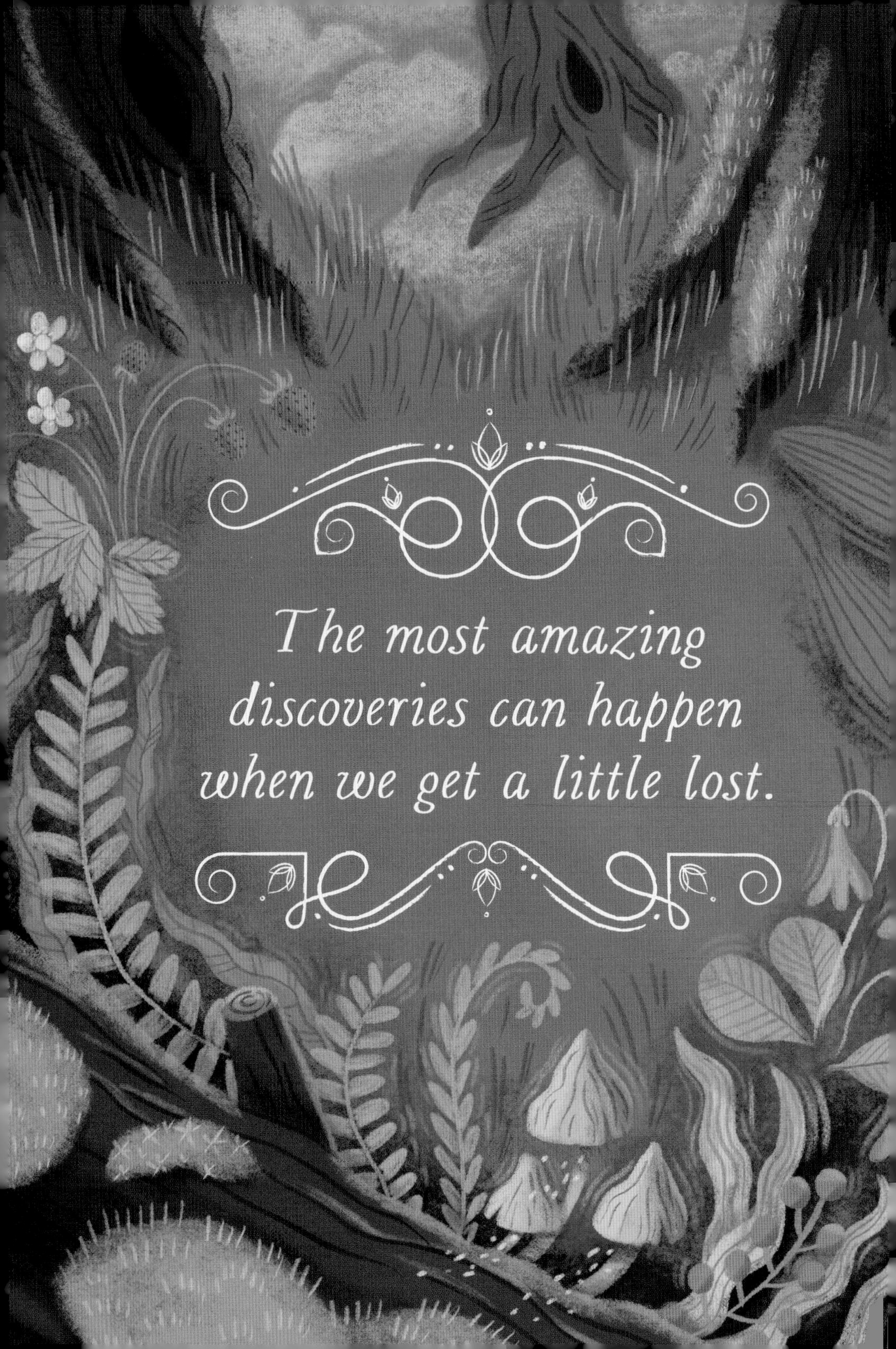
The most amazing
discoveries can happen
when we get a little lost.

Introduction:
A Brief History
of Magical Creatures

You might think you know everything about the woods around where you live—what kind of trails there are, if any, and what sorts of animals live there. And while you may have discovered a great deal already, this guide is here to encourage you to get out there and look again—and look closer—because there's something magical still to be found. You see, there are pockets of enchanted woods all around us, hidden among the ordinary; you could be out for a hike on a familiar trail, for instance, and realize that if you follow a strange path or make your own, you're suddenly in an area where magical creatures live right here on Earth, quietly existing alongside us. Of course, you might also run into an enchanted animal in the "ordinary" woods—they bring their magic with them wherever they go, after all. These magical creatures of the wood are a lot like the animals you already know, and some even share their common names—bear, trout, and wolf, for instance—but each looks a little different and has a special magical gift.

Let's talk a little more about what magical animals are. In general, they are caring citizens of the forest who get along well with ordinary animals and exist peacefully alongside them—except, of course, in the cases of animals who hunt other animals for food, which is a natural part of life whether magic is involved or not.

They have, based on what we know from the earliest accounts, been a part of our world for a very long time, perhaps as long as humans themselves have been here. They live in all different parts of the forest, from the treetops to caves to lakes and ponds, and many of them are caretakers of their surroundings or sometimes of other animals in the wood. Some of them are loved or feared by fairies, too. Many enchanted animals are shy and secretive, preferring to stay hidden in their pockets of magical woods and making themselves harder for researchers to locate. There are likely many undiscovered species out there still, waiting to be noticed by the right observer.

On the other hand, here is what magical animals of the wood *are not*: they are not spirit animals. A spirit animal, power animal, or totem animal, in the tradition of many Indigenous peoples, is a guardian spirit or guiding force in a person's life that takes the form of a particular animal. This protective spirit in animal form often has important lessons to offer the person it's associated with, and some of these animals stay with a person throughout their life, appearing in various ways at times when they most need guidance. This book does not cover animal guides—rather, we will be looking at living, breathing animals who have their own personalities, needs, and wants separate from any human and who happen to have some magical ability. However, if you're looking for a great resource on spirit animals instead, you might go to your library to search for books on animal guides or animal medicine. Just be sure you get an adult to help you find books written by the Indigenous people who are experts on this subject so that you get the right information.

In this guide, it's important to note that we will be focusing on animals who live in deciduous forests only—meaning, warmer or temperate forests that have trees whose leaves fall off in autumn and experience a range of seasons but without extremes in temperature. We won't be including any animals from boreal forests, which are colder and tend toward conifers like pine trees, or from the even warmer tropical rainforests, not because magical animals don't live there too—and in other habitats, from the mountains to the ocean—but simply because there are so many that those creatures would need their own book for us to have time to discuss them all!

Within the following pages you'll find plenty of information on the kinds of magical woodland creatures that researchers have already identified, as well as evidence of ones we're still learning about. This guide offers advice to help you spot these amazing creatures, interact with them safely, and recognize when you're in the presence of magic. You'll discover some helpful advice about how to walk in the woods in a way that earns these enchanted creatures' respect, an index of plants and flowers that are special to these amazing animals, a map of their magical woodland home, and even some crafts and quizzes to help bring you closer to their wild, wonderful world.

We hope this book helps bring some more magic into your life. So grab your hiking boots, a walking stick, and maybe a trusted friend, and let's go on a woodland adventure!

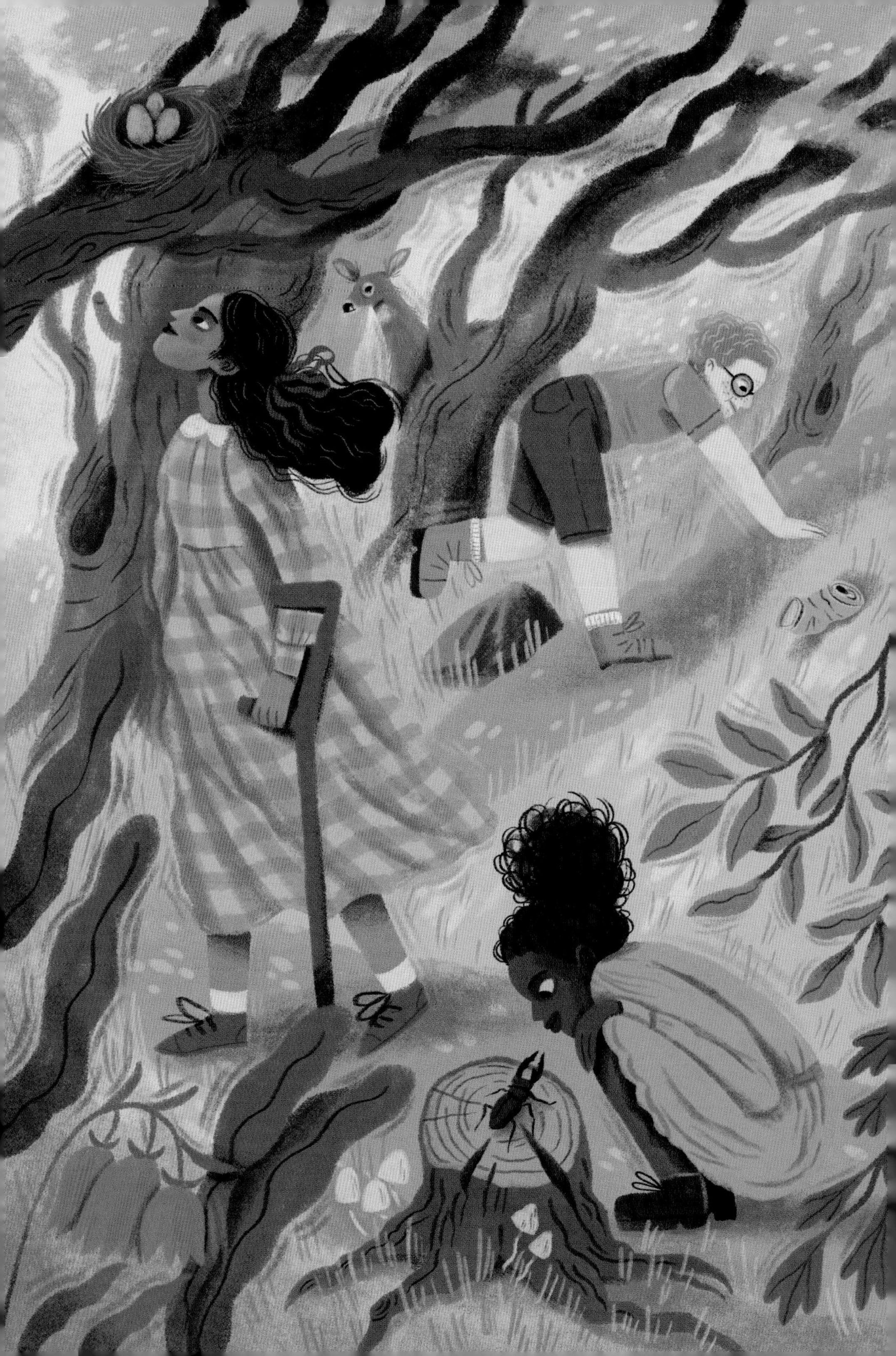

HOW TO WALK
IN THE WOODS

Whenever you're going into the woods—but especially when you're hoping to find a magical forest creature—it's important to the animals that you help take care of their environment. After all, you get to go home to a room that's made up just the way you like it, but the woods are their home and their cozy place. Magical creatures will only appear to those who show respect to their surroundings. In fact, being a kind custodian of the wood is a great way to get these creatures' attention for the right reasons. Below are some tips for your next day walk, hike, or camping trip so you can be a better friend to the wood and the animals in it.

LEAVE NO TRACE: This is the motto of the US National Park Service, and it's good advice to bring to any stretch of woods. It means leave no trash, don't take things home with you (unless you're directly given something, like a feather, by a magical creature), and try to stay on marked paths.

NEGATIVE TRACE: If you really want to go the extra mile for woodland animals, you can also pick up litter that others have left behind. Ask an adult for guidelines on how to do this safely, as some trash could be harmful to you as well.

KEEP YOUR DISTANCE: Always watch wildlife from a respectful distance. If you need instructions on getting closer to a certain animal, ask an adult for more help. A general rule is to stay about 100 yards away from large animals (the length of a football field or the height of the Statue of Liberty) and about 25 yards away from medium-sized animals (the length of a standard lap pool), but you should also trust your gut and the judgment of the adult with you.

LOOK WITH YOUR EYES, NOT WITH YOUR HANDS: Touching nests, dens, hives, and certain flowers and plants can upset creatures who will then smell that a human has been there and not want to come back to their homes. It can also be dangerous for both you and the animals who live there, so observing these places is best done with great care. And it goes without saying that you shouldn't necessarily touch any woodland creatures within your reach: Bees or spiders can sting and bite, and any mammal or bird that would allow you to get this close to them might be sick. Again, trust your gut and the judgment of the adult with you.

NO GRAFFITI: Painting on rocks and signs or carving into trees disturbs many animals' homes and leaves them looking for new places to live that aren't decorated in a way they didn't ask for.

WATCH WHERE YOU WALK: Sometimes, you'll really want or need to go off a marked trail, and when you do, the best way to be respectful to the wildlife and plants is to mind your steps so you aren't crushing fragile bugs or flowers or otherwise harming your surroundings.

CONNECT WITH OTHERS: Joining a scouting troop of some kind is a great way to get outdoors more with others who share your passion for the woods. You could also consider starting an environmental club at school to meet friends who want to go on more hikes and other woodland adventures.

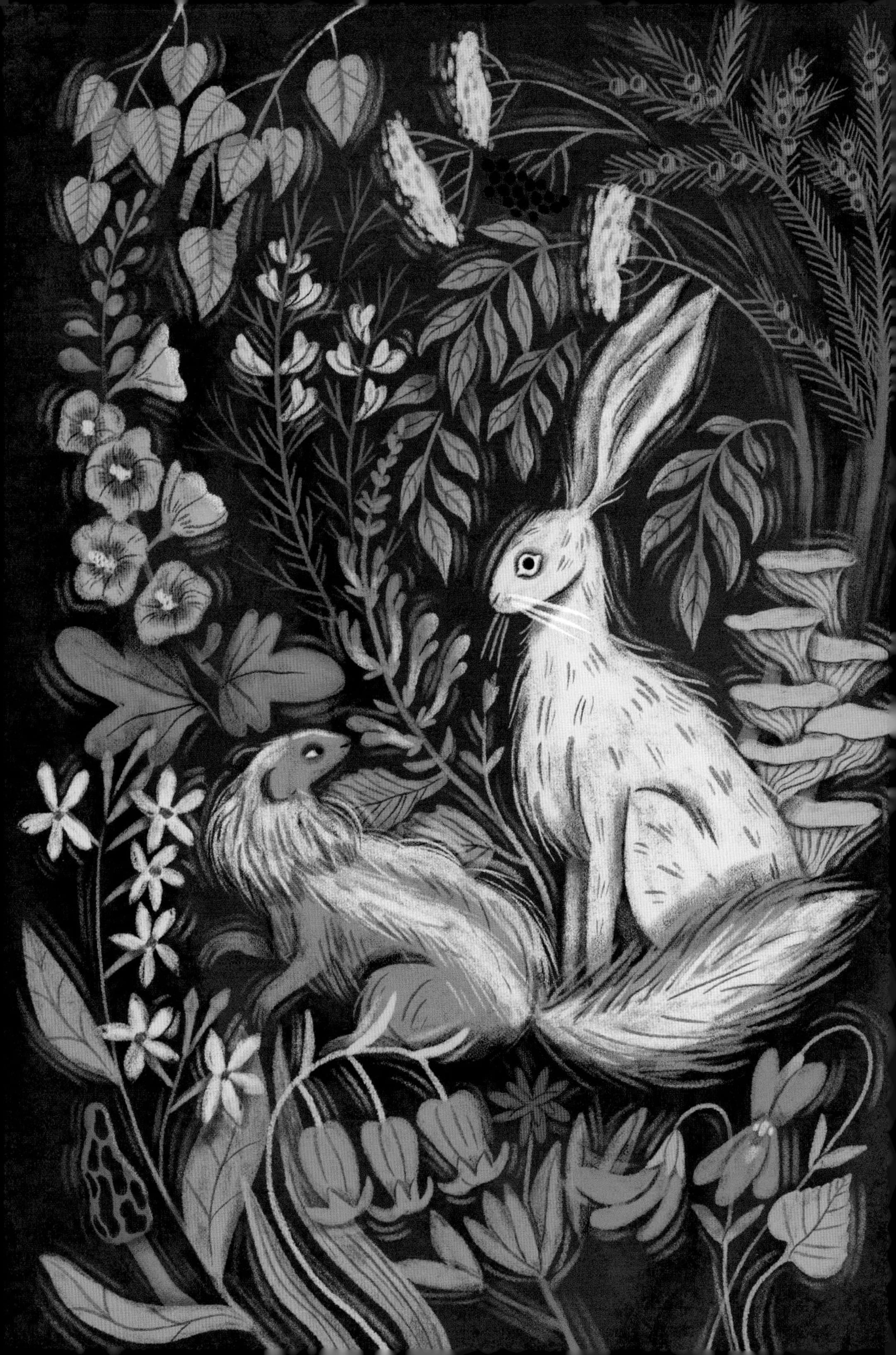

A MAGICAL HERBARIUM: PLANTS AND FLOWERS OF THE ENCHANTED WOOD

Welcome to the enchanted wood herbarium, a guide to the many trees, flowers, and herbs that have a special significance to the magical animals who live there—whether it's to provide shelter, food, or even care to the creatures who look after them. Being able to identify these growing things puts you one step closer to witnessing some magic. Just remember: be careful not to eat or touch any plant without adult supervision.

Flora

BLUEBELL: *A favorite of fairies, will also draw any magical creatures friendly to them*

BRAMBLE: *Provides delicious berries for most of the wood's herbivores*

COMMON DOG VIOLET: *Often gets the attention of enchanted butterflies*

COMMON GORSE: *Bright and cheerful, these flowers often attract enchanted bees*

NIGHT-BLOOMING JASMINE AND NIGHT-BLOOMING CEREUS: *Resting places of enchanted moths*

Fungi

BLACK TRUFFLE: *A favorite snack of enchanted wild boars*

CHANTERELLE: *Enchanted deer love to eat these*

HEDGEHOG MUSHROOM: *Some inhabitants of the wood, like chipmunks, treat these as pets*

MOREL: *Some egg-laying creatures hide their eggs in these*

OYSTER MUSHROOM: *Provides shelter during rain for smaller inhabitants of the wood*

Trees

BIRCH: *Enchanted woodpeckers bond with this tree*

ELDER: *Enchanted squirrels' favorite tree for grinding their teeth*

ELM: *The leaves of this tree are most often eaten by enchanted moose*

HOLLY: *Many enchanted animals use this tree's bright but poisonous berries for decorating dens and nests*

YEW: *Trees where enchanted spiders like to weave their webs*

Herbs

AMARANTH: *Used by some animals for healing*

HOLLYHOCK: *Employed by certain creatures to relieve itching*

LEMONGRASS: *This herb helps magical creatures relax*

SKULLCAP: *Worn as a decoration by some animals, while others use it as medicine*

STAR ANISE: *This potent herb increases certain creatures' magic when eaten*

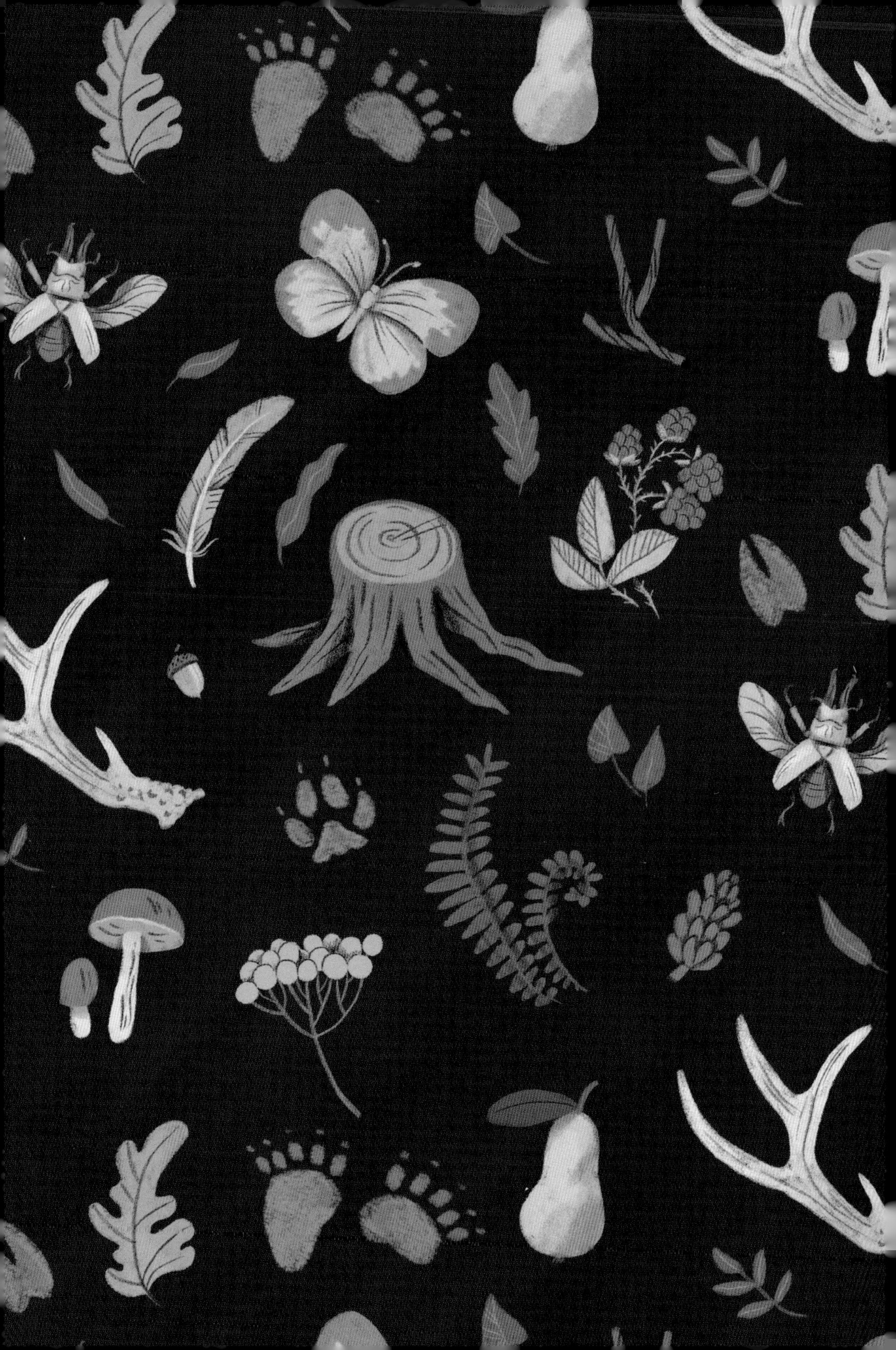

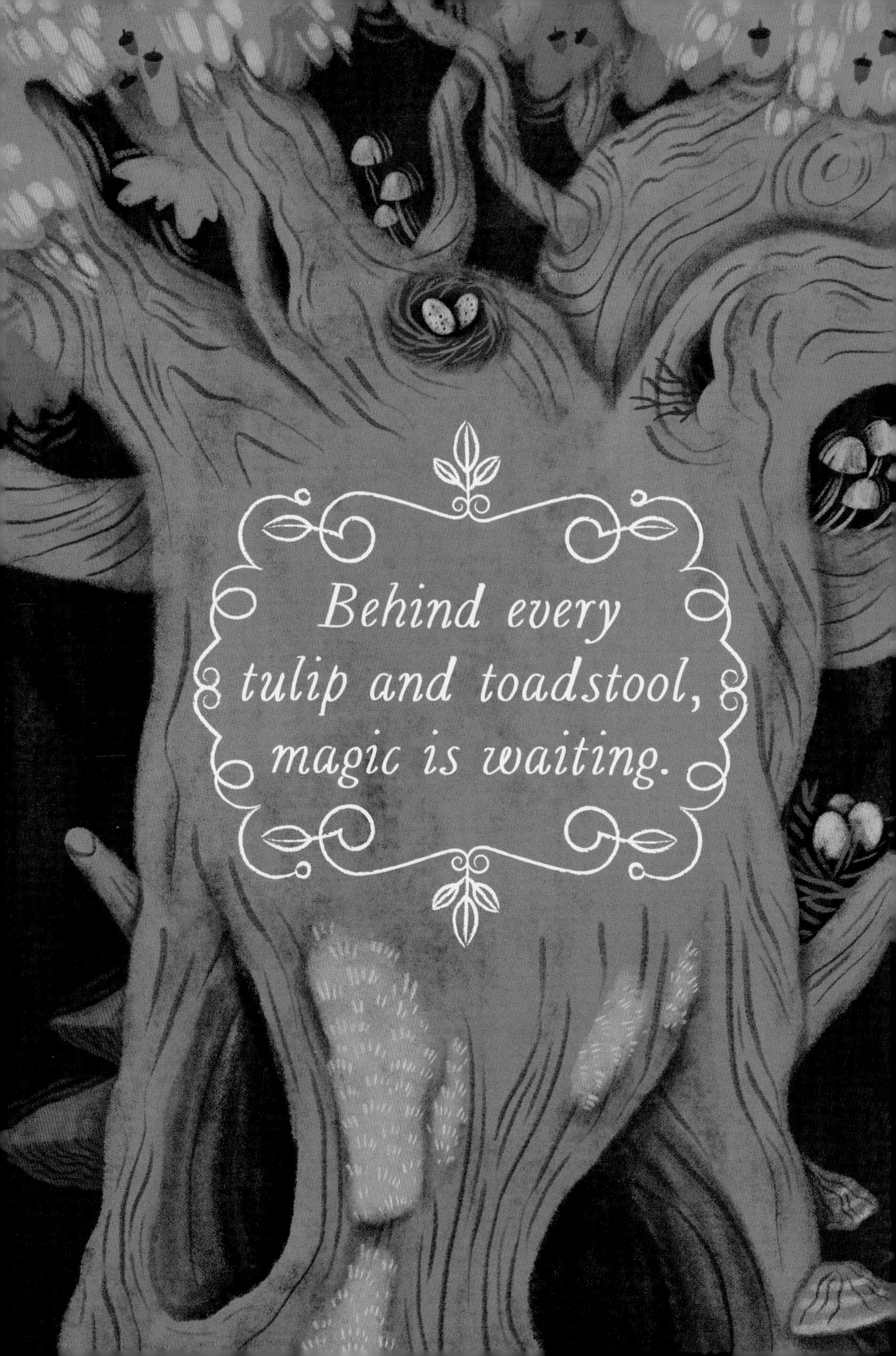
Behind every
tulip and toadstool,
magic is waiting.

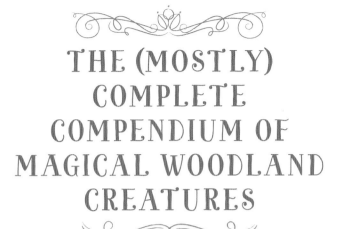

THE (MOSTLY)
COMPLETE
COMPENDIUM OF
MAGICAL WOODLAND
CREATURES

Although many magical creatures are already well-studied, there are also some that are shier and harder to find. Rest assured, researchers are always at work searching for these more elusive animals, gathering evidence through fossils, tracks, and firsthand accounts, as well as doing fieldwork—heading out into the forest in the hope of discovering an enchanted area of the woods where they might be able to observe these amazing animals in their natural habitats.

They do this important work at all hours—from sunrise to sundown, and even through the night, because just like ordinary animals, some magical creatures are *diurnal* (active during the day), while others are *nocturnal* (active at night), and many more are *crepuscular* (most active at dawn and dusk).

We've organized this guide mostly by the animals' class: a scientific way of grouping like creatures together. You might recognize familiar terms like *mammal* and *arthropod* from science class, and you may find that many of these animals look and sound familiar—with some slight but notable differences, of course. Scientific names for magical animals are, after all, inspired by ones for real animals, but they don't follow an identical naming structure. In these pages, you'll find information on each creature's diet, personality, appearance, and what sort of magic they might share with you.

We hope this guide will inspire you to get out into the woods around your home to explore more often—always with adult supervision, of course. You may even want to carry a journal to take notes on any evidence you find on your adventures. As always, don't forget to appreciate the hidden magic that lives all around us!

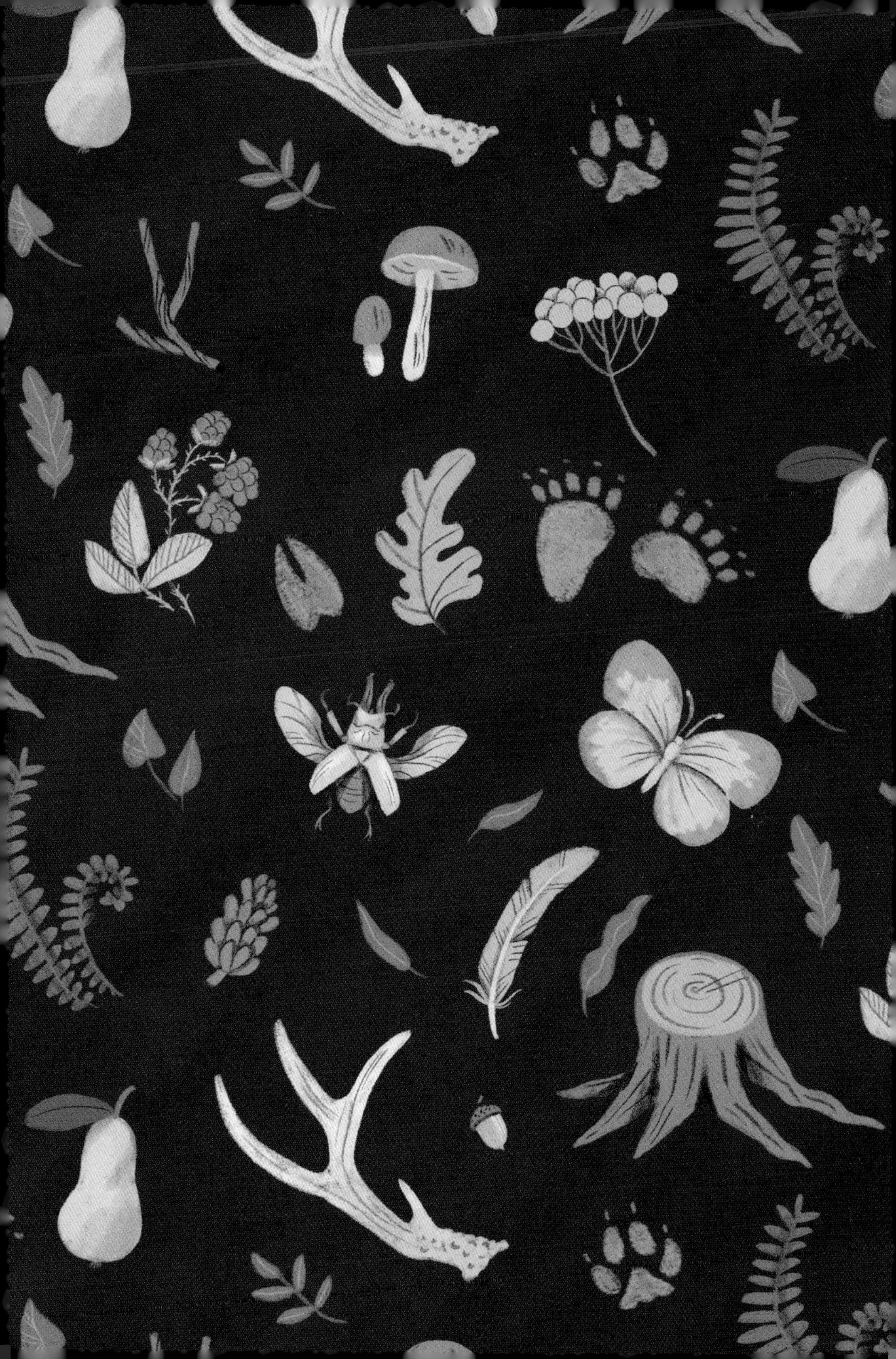

Mammals

BATS

SCIENTIFIC NAME: *Chiroptera enchanta*
HABITAT/RANGE: Caves and treetops, when hunting
DIET: Varies by subspecies; some herbivore, some carnivore
SIZE: Extra-small to large, by subspecies;
wingspan ranges from 5 inches to 5 feet
ACTIVE TIME: Nocturnal

These bats aren't difficult to spot once they've come awake for the night, mainly because they travel in large flocks or *coffins*, a playful term that researchers have coined for a group of enchanted bats. Much like migratory birds, these bats become active in large numbers each night and never stray too far from the group unless something is wrong. They vary greatly in size between subspecies, with some being only about as large as a human thumb and others more closely resembling small dogs flapping through the air. They come in many colors as well across subspecies—often white, but also soft beige, pale pink, or jet-black. They all have gold-veined wings, which help distinguish them from ordinary bats even in the dark, as well as large amber eyes. They're known for tucking flowers or sprigs of berries behind their ears to let other bats know which coffin they belong to. They have sometimes been observed tossing these flowers, berries, and other bits of forest debris back and forth through the air as they play and catch their meals—be it bugs or pollen and sweet nectar—while flitting among the treetops.

Enchanted bats know the forest from top to bottom better than anyone, even the sharp-eyed enchanted eagles. Each group of bats has its own unique playlist of songs, and there's some magic in their vocals. Unlike ordinary bats, who use echolocation to find objects and food in the dark—a process where sound waves bouncing back off of objects tell the bats what it is—enchanted bats use their singing to map the entire area of forest where they're flying, able to "see" everything from fallen leaves on the forest floor to worms and birds up in the tree branches all at once and in great detail.

Just like these bats know that they belong with their group, they understand that people belong with other people and pets. If approached for assistance, they can help locate a lost hiker or lost pet that might be roaming the woods thanks to their quick and thorough magical song-mapping.

BEARS

SCIENTIFIC NAME: *Ursidae enchanta*
HABITAT/RANGE: Throughout the forest,
preferring higher elevations with rocks and caves
DIET: Herbivore, love eating dandelions, nuts, berries
SIZE: Large, 4 feet tall at the shoulder, 7 feet long
ACTIVE TIME: Crepuscular

As with any wild animal you meet in the woods, it's important to view bears with caution and from a safe distance. Yet even from far away, it's possible to realize that you're in the presence of a magical bear because of the greater variety of colors to their fur, such as white, cream, and sunset orange. The size of these creatures is another giveaway—they are easily as long and tall as a large grizzly bear. However, these bears' gentleness comes with a quiet strength, and they are known for being fiercely protective of any creature—bear or fairy or otherwise—they consider to be part of their family. They value the comforts of their forest home (usually a cozy cave known as a *den*), which they decorate with flowers and pine cones and other trinkets that strike their fancy.

Bears are known for their nurturing ways, and cubs live with their parents well into adulthood. So, while you may glimpse a lone bear in the wild, chances are high that the rest of their family is somewhere nearby. What *is* understood about their magic so far is that it seems to come from their vocalizations—when they grumble, any bees nearby will swarm and lead the bears to their hive for a taste of delicious honey. And when they roar, the fierce sound makes a certain area of the forest impossible to enter for a period of some hours, which one surprised researcher discovered while out on a bird-watching hike with his friends. He heard the familiar sound of a bear, and suddenly, he couldn't take another step forward into the trees no matter what he did even though the pathway ahead of him looked clear.

But that's not all: researchers believe that the bears' roars also inspire courage in anyone who has entered the forest with good intentions.

BEAVERS

SCIENTIFIC NAME: *Castor enchanta*
HABITAT/RANGE: Near water
DIET: Herbivore, mostly twigs and saplings
SIZE: Medium, 3–4 feet including tail
ACTIVE TIME: All the time

These hard workers can be spotted in the forest night or day—they rarely sleep, because there's simply too much to do, although they take periods of rest in the afternoon where they disappear beneath the water and into their castle-like dens to close their eyes for a few hours. While these enchanted beavers might at first closely resemble their ordinary cousins, a longer look in the sunlight or moonlight will reveal the way their tails sparkle; this is where researchers believe they store their magic. Like ordinary beavers, they are strong swimmers, though they don't often indulge in a long swim for fun. Instead, they use this skill to keep working even when the water they inhabit is running fast from a storm.

One of the easiest ways to know you're in the presence of an enchanted beaver is by studying their den. The homes they build are far more elaborate than those of ordinary beavers and might have several rooms within them either above or beneath the water. This is helpful, as these beavers like to live in large family groups and age slowly, so grandparents can be sure to have rooms away from small children and everyone gets their own quiet space. Another way to tell an enchanted beaver from an ordinary one is by the scent they leave where they work: there's a smell of wildflowers and dewy meadow grass on the trees they use for their latest project. (They're always trying to upgrade their living spaces.)

If you approach one of these creatures' homes and ask nicely, you might find yourself gifted with a stick from their pile. While these beavers work hard to make their own success, carrying one of their twigs around will bring you luck for an entire day, and might just inspire you to try to make some of your own success once that luck runs out.

CHIPMUNKS

SCIENTIFIC NAME: *Tamias enchanta*
HABITAT/RANGE: All over the forest
DIET: Omnivore, love nuts and bird eggs
SIZE: Small, up to 7 inches long
ACTIVE TIME: Diurnal

These enchanted chipmunks may be small, but they don't lack for big personalities and a great sense of adventure. While ordinary chipmunks have stripes of black and white on their backs, their magical cousins only appear to look the same until they scurry into the sunlight, which turns their stripes to sparkling silver and gold. Their eyes are usually yellow, but can also be fiery orange or deep scarlet, and they don't seem to be harmed by staring directly into the sun. In fact, researchers have noted that sunbathing is important to these chipmunks somehow, almost as if it's as necessary to them as eating or sleeping. They have never been seen on a gray or rainy day in the ordinary forest, which must mean they retreat to a more magical part of the wood when the weather here doesn't suit them.

Thanks to their love of exploring, these chipmunks can be found all over any forest—they want to climb, see, and taste everything that the wood has to offer. They can get along with just about any other creature, magical or not, and they'll eat any food that's put in front of them (and sometimes, if campers have left behind trash, some nonfood items as well). Of course, they don't have to eat your forgotten hair ties or tissues—their magic lets them turn any food they hold between their paws into something else, like an acorn into a beetle if that's what they're in the mood for. They travel in packs, chatting and laughing the day away, which can sometimes annoy certain animals who prefer their peace and quiet—researchers have noticed that these chipmunks seem to be a favorite snack for enchanted cougars in particular. Curiously, however, the cougars have been observed gagging and making faces after swallowing one of these little creatures, which has led researchers to suspect that enchanted chipmunks must taste rather spicy.

COUGARS

SCIENTIFIC NAME: *Puma enchanta*
HABITAT/RANGE: Rocky areas of forest, highly territorial
DIET: Carnivore, prey on small magic and nonmagic creatures
SIZE: Large, about 7 feet long and 2–3 feet tall
ACTIVE TIME: Crepuscular

While these enchanted cougars have never been known to attack humans, researchers recommend admiring them only from a safe distance. They're most often found at higher areas in the forest, like rocky hills from which they can keep an eye on the trees below. You'll never see more than one magical cougar in a given area, because just like ordinary cougars, they are highly territorial and proud of the part of the forest they protect. You're most likely to spot one of these beautiful, enchanted hunters if you're out in the woods at dusk or dawn. Periods of low light are when they search for food and survey their kingdom-of-sorts. A magical cougar can be recognized even from a distance by their fur, which is slightly longer than that of ordinary cougars and glows gently as if lit from within. The glow is brighter after they've had a particularly satisfying meal and dimmer when they're hungry or sick or tired. Their eyes—as noted by the few researchers who have gotten close enough to observe them—can be any color from violet to neon yellow, and it's suspected that the hue changes to reflect their mood.

Enchanted cougars may wander alone, but they have a playful nature just the same. They can jump up to twenty feet in the air and leap across a distance of up to forty feet. They are often spotted sitting peacefully on some rock or other at the end of a hunt, resting their lean, muscular bodies and taking in a sunrise or moonrise before retiring for a little sleep. You won't find many stronger magical animals in the woods than the cougar, whether in body, mind, or spirit. Their magic is especially powerful, and it's what makes them worth more than just a brief look for anyone who happens across them. Spotting an enchanted cougar can heal a person's broken heart and even make it stronger—something researchers have so far found difficult to measure, though each one has noted that their deepest sadness faded after being in the presence of these creatures.

DEER

SCIENTIFIC NAME: *Cervidae enchanta*
HABITAT/RANGE: Often found in meadows and along streams
DIET: Herbivore, prefer flowers and certain mushrooms
SIZE: Medium, about 3 feet tall at the shoulder
ACTIVE TIME: Diurnal

If you're ever on a hike and feel like you're being watched in the woods, you probably are—by a herd of these sweet and especially beautiful enchanted deer. They're slightly smaller than ordinary deer, a difference that's hard to notice without getting closer than these creatures would prefer. They also have the reddish-brown coloring you'd expect to see on ordinary deer, and like some non-magical varieties, their coats are flecked with spots of white; that is, until the sunlight hits their fur. A direct beam of sun will reveal whether the white-spotted deer you've discovered is magical or not, as it will turn the seemingly white spots on an enchanted deer to their true color: blue, pink, yellow, and even rainbow are some color patterns researchers have noted so far.

Like many creatures who come from the magical woods hidden all around us, these deer are particularly shy when approached by strangers, which is why they're so aware of their surroundings at all times. They tend to travel in family groups of thirty to forty at a time in winter and spring, helping each other search for things to eat when food is scarce, although in the summer they might wander with just a handful of others for company. Luckily, their magic allows them to walk in the woods undetected, completely disappearing from view even in the presence of campers or backpackers. They can even pass by without making a sound or leaving any hoofprints to track. On the rare occasion that you do discover a herd of these deer wandering in a meadow (their preferred place to roam while they snack on wildflowers) and manage to make eye contact with one of these gentle creatures, they might share their magical gift with you by turning you invisible for a few hours with a twitch of their nose or tail.

FOXES

SCIENTIFIC NAME: *Vulpes enchanta*

HABITAT/RANGE: All over, often found beneath the trees or in rocky outcroppings

DIET: Omnivore, known for stealing human snack foods

SIZE: Small, about 20 inches long and 15 inches tall

ACTIVE TIME: Nocturnal

Just like ordinary foxes, enchanted foxes are most active at night, so this is an animal that's easier to spot if you're camping in a forest somewhere. Unlike ordinary foxes, however, they have a much stronger appetite for human snack foods. (Researchers have noted that beef jerky sticks, dried fruit, and trail mix are all popular with enchanted foxes, although they seem to be able to barely tolerate other snacks like chips.) These foxes tend to be on the smaller side, just slightly larger than a fennec fox when compared to other ordinary fox species. It can be difficult to tell in the dark unless you have bright moonlight or a flashlight handy, but their fur ranges in color from dusky purple to deep indigo, taking on the different hues of the night sky. Occasionally, you'll see one of these foxes with a sprinkling of white dots across their back like their fur has formed the pattern of a constellation.

If you're unable to find a good light source and come across a fox, another way to tell whether they're enchanted is by their calls—magical foxes have cries that are more like singing than an ordinary fox's screams and howls. There's a certain repeated melody to every sound they make, and sometimes, you'll even catch one laughing. Enchanted foxes are some of the wisest creatures in the magical woods; in fact, that's their magic. They know a great many things, from how airplanes stay up to how to solve most questions on a math test, but they also love a good joke among their friends and will often play pranks on one another. These foxes are not shy, and research has shown that if you find and befriend one, they'll tell you the answer to any one question you ask—so choose wisely, especially if you have a difficult test coming up.

HEDGEHOGS

SCIENTIFIC NAME: *Erinaceidae enchanta*
HABITAT/RANGE: Forest floor, meadows, along streams
DIET: Omnivore, love mosquitoes
SIZE: Small, about 8 inches long
ACTIVE TIME: Nocturnal

The most colorful of the wood's enchanted creatures seem to come out only at night, and the magical hedgehog is no exception. While they are roughly the same size, weight, and shape as an ordinary hedgehog, once spotted, their appearance is an easy giveaway that you've stumbled onto something enchanted. Rather than the usual brown fur, these creatures come in a variety of pastel colors like blue, pink, purple, yellow, and green, or occasionally a silver so pale it might be mistaken for white. You can often see magical hedgehogs along the banks of streams or lakes in the early evening, emerging from their sleep to feast on the mosquitoes that like to gather near water. Of course, they'll just as happily eat leaves, ferns, and flowers, and they often keep these snacks right on their quills. Being rather shy by nature, they often decorate their quills with twigs and plant matter to better blend in with their forest surroundings and avoid being discovered by people or other creatures.

Unlike ordinary hedgehogs, who prefer to be alone, enchanted hedgehogs like to sleep piled up with their friends for warmth in cozy dens and can be seen playing and barking at one another by the light of the full moon—their favorite time to gather. These powerful and prickly balls of joy have a magic that can be shared with humans: researchers have recently found that if a magical hedgehog willingly gives you one of their quills, you'll be protected from negative energies and ill will as long as you carry it with you. Of course, as a few rather unlucky researchers also learned, you should never try to take one of their quills without it being offered to you, even if it's lying on the ground—that leads to all sorts of bad luck.

MOOSE

SCIENTIFIC NAME: *Alces enchanta*
HABITAT/RANGE: Areas near water; warm, sunny meadows
DIET: Herbivore, love acorns and fresh leaves on trees
SIZE: Extra-large, 7 feet tall at the shoulder
ACTIVE TIME: Crepuscular

One of the surest ways to tell that you're in the presence of a magical moose is to wait for sunlight to touch their antlers, which glimmer pearly white when exposed to sun. Their fur comes in a wider range of colors as well, such as white, black, crimson, and deep evergreen. Their coats are also thinner than that of an ordinary moose, which allows them to tolerate warmer temperatures and live in a wider range of forests than nonmagic types. Researchers suspect that the area of the magical wood where they're born must be particularly warm, as these moose love to lay around for hours sunbathing in quiet meadows. They've also been spotted rolling through the flowers in spring and summer and basking on rocks near water where they can take a dip if they get a little too hot.

While they may love warmer weather, they're not at all hot-tempered—as ordinary moose can sometimes be. Enchanted moose are calm, wise creatures who consider every step before they take it. This may not make them one of the fastest animals in the wood, but it certainly makes them among the most thought-ful. And it's a good thing, too, because their magic lies in their hoofbeats: they can clear a path through an impassable part of the forest with just a single stomp, rearranging where trees are growing and where that little hiking path is leading so that everyone can reach destinations that were once impossible. Researchers have observed throughout the years that other creatures—magical and nonmagical alike—are drawn to enchanted moose and the possi-bilities that they create with their magic; it's not uncommon to see a moose surrounded by a hovering cloud of butterflies, dragonflies, or even some of the smaller fairies like sprites who sometimes visit the woods or being followed at a respectful distance by a magical cougar or wolf pack seeking new territory. Anyone looking to make changes in their life might hope to spot an enchanted moose so they can ask for help in clearing the way to new opportunities.

OTTERS

SCIENTIFIC NAME: *Lutrinae enchanta*
HABITAT/RANGE: Rivers, streams, lakes
DIET: Carnivore, prefer fish and snails and bubble sprites
SIZE: Medium, 2–4 feet in length
ACTIVE TIME: Diurnal

Meet one of the most playful creatures in the magical wood: enchanted otters! Researchers are not yet sure whether these otters even age, because they never stop acting like young pups. They spend their days doing tricks and laughing at the silliest jokes—told to each other in their special language that sounds a lot like dogs barking. Enchanted otters come in many sizes, ranging in length from two to four feet, which leads researchers to suspect there are several subspecies. Unlike ordinary otters, their fur never really gets wet, and their eyes are always river-blue. But even from a distance, you might be able to tell you're in the presence of a magical otter because of the necklaces of shells they collect and wear on strings of kelp or other aquatic plants. They seem to use these small shells as a sort of currency, or maybe they trade them just for fun—more research is needed.

These otters are strong swimmers and are always found around a body of water, whether that's a pond or stream. Their magic is in their ability to create cheer—they make every person who catches sight of them laugh uncontrollably for the rest of the day. One researcher learned this when she was studying bubble sprites by a river running through the woods behind her home and found two otters catching the little fairies and eating them. She *wanted* to be upset that her research subjects were being eaten, but all she could do was giggle. She was still laughing when one of the otters splashed her and sped away, and even laughed through doing all her work that night. The next morning, she felt inspired to take a painting class: something she had always loved doing as a young girl.

POSSUMS

SCIENTIFIC NAME: *Didelphis enchanta*
HABITAT/RANGE: Most often found in trees
with plenty of branches
DIET: Omnivore, prefer fruit when possible
SIZE: Medium, up to 3 feet long and up to 1.5 feet tall
ACTIVE TIME: Nocturnal

If you see a possum scurrying around at night that looks bathed
in silver or blue or pale pink by the light of the moon, your eyes
aren't playing tricks on you. That's a magical possum, a solitary
but gentle creature who, much like the enchanted raccoon, is an
expert climber and mover who isn't afraid to sometimes stray out of
the forest in search of new things to eat or things that need to be
found. These possums come in a wide array of fur colors found in
nature, while their tails are most often a pale gold or silver. Much
like their ordinary cousins, they also have an opposable thumb that
helps them pick flowers or sort through a trash pile.

Where magical raccoons can help someone find what's missing from their life, magical possums are experts at finding your lost items. Researchers have seen them locate homework pages that were due months ago, lost action figures that have been sorely missed, and even smartphones that seemed to have grown legs and walked off somewhere. Though further study is needed, it's believed they use their tails to lead them to missing belongings much like a human might use a metal detector to search for lost coins or other treasures. These possums will expect something in terms of payment, of course: fresh fruit or vegetables will do nicely, but if you don't have any of those in your kitchen, there's not a snack food they've turned their noses up at yet. In fact, they're known to have great memories and will often revisit a place where they've received a favorite meal. So if you're prone to losing things, be sure to keep some extra treats to share, and an enchanted possum could become your regular visitor.

RABBITS

SCIENTIFIC NAME: *Leporidae enchanta*
HABITAT/RANGE: All over the forest, but especially meadows
DIET: Omnivore, love dandelions
SIZE: Medium, usually about 20 inches tall
ACTIVE TIME: Nocturnal

These rabbits can be difficult to spot unless you're camping in the woods overnight or staying out late to have a bonfire and s'mores with family and friends or a scouting troop because they are especially active at night. These rabbits are on the larger side, and while their fur tends to be ordinary coat colors like brown, gray, and white, there are also enchanted rabbits whose fur is a dusky purple or a buttery yellow. Their ears are slightly longer than those of normal rabbits, dragging on the ground as they hop along on their nightly errands. Researchers have discovered that these extra-long ears serve an important purpose for enchanted rabbits: they twist them into different shapes and symbols, which is how they safely and silently communicate with each other. Currently, a team of researchers is trying to complete an index of all the different ear positions and their meanings to better understand what they are saying.

Like the enchanted deer, these rabbits travel in large family groups at certain times of the year and are almost never seen alone. Though further research is needed, their magic seems to be stronger the more rabbits are around. Sometimes, an ordinary rabbit who's become separated from their family will join an enchanted nest (or family group) and, as has been observed on at least one occasion, learn some of the ear-shaping language to communicate with their new magical friends.

Magical rabbits are a challenge to find because their magic is their speed. You might think you see a butter-yellow rabbit outside your tent, but before you can grab a flashlight or pull out your phone to take a picture, it's already gone, leaving you to wonder if you really saw anything at all. If you're lucky enough to stumble onto one of the small paths carved out by these rabbits who know the woods so well, whether by day or at night, it will take you where you're trying to go much faster than the usual hiking trails on a human's map.

RACCOONS

SCIENTIFIC NAME: *Procyon enchanta*
HABITAT/RANGE: Most often found near water
DIET: Omnivore, like coffee and compost piles
SIZE: Medium, about 4 feet long
ACTIVE TIME: Nocturnal

These raccoons are slightly larger than ordinary ones, and while they otherwise look much the same with their whiskered faces and ringed tails, they come in a greater variety of fur colors and patterns. Some have more elaborate masks around their eyes, while others have simpler ones; some even have thin circles of dark fur that look almost like human glasses. This seems fitting for these solitary magical creatures, as researchers have found them to be exceptionally smart. They're known for figuring out how to climb and sneak into the most difficult, well-guarded places, especially if one of their favorite foods is involved—like the eggs of a magical woodpecker or goshawk. They are strong swimmers as well as climbers, and these enchanted raccoons can see for miles in the dark.

Although magical raccoons make their home in the woods and are most often found near water, they are bolder than many other magical species—and willing to leave the forest on occasion. This isn't just because they enjoy sneaking into human neighborhoods for a taste of delicacies (some of their favorites being coffee grounds and compost piles). These raccoons have a passion for both the natural world and all things human-made, and they understand that humans throw out some of the most interesting things, which aren't trash at all. For instance, a sweater full of holes still makes a cozy nest, and a busted backpack can haul their next meal and other treasures back to the forest.

These clever, dumpster-diving creatures are also the magical detectives of the wood: they have the ability to help you find whatever is missing in your life—an undiscovered talent, a great new friendship, or a hobby you'll love, for instance—when approached with respect and kindness. They bring their same passion for treats and trash to their detective work, searching fearlessly through your life and looking in the difficult places that no one else is willing to. They aren't afraid of a room that hasn't been cleaned in many weekends or a chaotic life any more than they are the grossest garbage cans or the muddiest pools.

SKUNKS

SCIENTIFIC NAME: *Mephitis enchanta*

HABITAT/RANGE: Edges of the wood, hollow
logs, and woodpiles

DIET: Omnivore, but bugs and acorns are favorites

SIZE: Small, up to 2 feet long

ACTIVE TIME: Nocturnal

What's that smell? If it's something particularly nasty, you can be sure that's not an enchanted skunk but an ordinary one. These beautiful skunks come in a wide array of natural colors, such as white, russet red, gray, deep brown, and black. Enchanted skunks have larger eyes than ordinary ones and a thick ruff of white fur around their necks where they often keep a collection of sweet-smelling flowers that they've picked with their claws to inspire them to create beautiful new scents. (They use the fifth opposable claw on their paws much like humans use our thumbs.) These skunks have very sensitive noses, so come moonrise, they wake up and start sniffing out the most enchanting aromas the forest has to offer; they won't eat anything that doesn't smell good to them and will avoid areas where unpleasant odors like mud or pond scum have built up for too long.

With their ability to follow their noses to only the best foods and experiences, enchanted skunks are almost always cheerful. They love to play and create, and they're most known for spreading their good cheer through the scents they spray over their favorite territories. If you're in a quiet part of the forest and suddenly smell a wonderful combination of falling leaves, the earth after it rains, and sun-touched flowers just opening their petals, chances are an enchanted skunk has recently been by to fill the area with the scent of their magical home. You might even find yourself in a much better mood just by staying and breathing in the aroma for a while. And if the enchanted skunk is still nearby and happens to notice you, you might be lucky enough to experience some of their magic for yourself—they can also create and spray your favorite scents, like hot chocolate or birthday cake or baking bread, to remind you of happy times.

SQUIRRELS

SCIENTIFIC NAME: *Sciurus enchanta*
HABITAT/RANGE: Most often found up in the trees
DIET: Omnivore, love crunchy insects and nuts
SIZE: Small, about 15 inches long
ACTIVE TIME: Diurnal

While you might think that squirrel above your head is an ordinary one, look again, paying special attention to the length and shape of their tail. While magical squirrels come in ordinary colors, their tails are anything but. Longer than the tails of normal squirrels and extra fluffy, the shape of an enchanted squirrels' tail marks it as one of several subspecies. Their tails are also what allow them to fly between trees—not glide, like ordinary "flying squirrels" do with their extra folds of skin. No, enchanted squirrels are able to make themselves fully airborne and stay that way for as long as they like, although they do eventually get tired and need to find a branch where they can rest. Researchers have even observed them doing aerial acrobatics on several occasions, adding rolls midflight or zooming up to the top of a tree with incredible zip and then diving back down again as if for fun.

Though they love to play when in the air, these magical squirrels are most often spotted among the forest branches, working hard to provide food for themselves, their families, and every other woodland creature who eats plants and flowers. After all, they know that winter is never truly far off, and they don't want anyone going hungry. Like the teeth of ordinary squirrels, theirs never stop growing, a problem that's solved by the way they gnaw on tree bark, grinding their teeth to a manageable length as they work on their harvest. You see, flight isn't the creatures' only magic, or their most important. When they drop the nuts and seeds that they've gathered as they scurry and fly around the forest, those little seeds take root immediately, helping new plants grow that will provide food for other creatures—magic and nonmagic alike—to enjoy in time.

WILD BOARS

SCIENTIFIC NAME: *Sus enchanta*

HABITAT/RANGE: Sometimes meadows;
sometimes cool, shady places

DIET: Omnivore, though they prefer plants and fungi

SIZE: Large, up to 6 feet long and
3–4 feet high at the shoulder

ACTIVE TIME: Nocturnal

Though these enchanted boars only come out at night like their ordinary cousins, it's difficult to miss them when they do. Their tusks are longer than those of normal boars and come in many beautiful metallic colors from gold to silver to copper that change depending on their mood. Researchers believe gold means they're happy or at least content, silver means they're doing okay or getting restless, and copper means they're in a very bad mood and looking for a fight. Mostly, though, enchanted boars get along well with one another—in fact, they're rarely seen out of the company of other boars, preferring to travel and forage and swim in packs. Enchanted boars are graceful in the water, and if they're not out grazing on fresh wildflowers in a meadow, they're often found in cool, shady places near larger bodies of water where they can go for a swim as a herd.

Their tusks don't just tell researchers about their moods, however; they also hold all of an enchanted boar's magic, so it's important to them to protect their tusks during confrontations with other boars or more often other creatures who might be competing with them for swimming space or food. There are few magical animals as confident and assertive as enchanted boars, and they've been known to start fires when they don't get their way—they can create flames when they stomp the ground with their hooves, which of course poses a danger to any dry area of forest where a wildfire can quickly take hold. It's a good thing that enchanted boars' hotheaded nature and fire-starting abilities are well-known among other creatures, both magic and nonmagic alike! Most of the time, other animals go out of their way to make sure these boars are able to keep their cool so everyone stays safe.

WOLVES

SCIENTIFIC NAME: *Canis lupus enchanta*
HABITAT/RANGE: All over the forest
DIET: Carnivore, mostly
SIZE: Medium, about 5 feet long, 2.5 feet tall
ACTIVE TIME: Nocturnal

Another magical creature easily told apart from its ordinary counter-part, enchanted wolves only come out at night, when the shadows make it easier to hide their otherwise very noticeable appearance from any who might wish to interrupt their routines. Of course, all it takes is a little moonlight to see that these wolves are special: their fur is most often white, though it can occasionally be shades of blue or red or purple, and they have butterfly-like antennae sprouting from their heads just behind their ears that are as pale as the moon itself. Researchers currently believe that these antennae help the wolves sense the best path when they're running through the forest on a hunt or playing a game with their pack. And it's well-known that these wolves love to play. They are also fiercely loyal to their pack, and each one gets along so well with the others that when they sing to the moon, every wolf stays in perfect harmony.

Although magical wolves are primarily carnivores, preferring to leap into the air to catch fireflies and moths with their long tongues or snack on squirrels and other small game they chase through the wood, it's been observed that a few of these enchanted creatures have developed a taste for something a little sweeter—marshmallows roasted over a campfire. The smell is always sure to draw them, so if you happen to be camping and making s'mores, take a look into the trees around you and you just might spot a pack of magical wolves running past, tongues lolling out to catch the smoky-sweet scent of roasting marshmallows in the air as they hurry after their next meal or adventure—clearing fallen trees and jumping over steep ravines without a care thanks to their magic that allows the whole pack to leap over any obstacle in their path when they're in pursuit of a common goal.

Reptiles

LIZARDS

SCIENTIFIC NAME: *Squamata enchanta*
HABITAT/RANGE: Mostly in trees, near stream banks
DIET: Carnivore, prefer insects but will snack on sprites
SIZE: Small, from 2 inches to 2 feet long (not counting tail)
ACTIVE TIME: Diurnal

Just like ordinary lizards, these enchanted lizards come in many different sizes, colors, and shapes. Their scales are often as bright as the magical forest they live in: neon shades of pink, purple, and blue being especially common. These lizards all have long tongues, which help them catch bugs out of the air—of course, they sometimes mistake a bubble sprite or other small fairy for a mosquito or fly and swallow it just the same. Enchanted lizards also all share a common feature of small horns on the tops of their heads. Just as with enchanted snakes, researchers believe this points to a common ancestor with dragons somewhere far back in their history.

When they aren't down near a creek hunting for bugs or tiny fish, they are most often spotted high up in trees, where there are usually other bugs to catch, like enchanted butterflies. Their extra-long curly tails help them swing from tree to tree almost as if flying. And just like their ordinary cousins, they can detach their tails if they feel threatened, allowing them a few extra seconds to escape.

These lizards are known for lounging in a particular tree all day, leading researchers to suspect they love being lazy even though they never get sick or tired. While they can eventually die of old age or become prey to magical hedgehogs or other hunters, these lizards are immune to all diseases carried by animals and humans alike. This immunity is believed to be their strongest magic, and they can share this protection from sickness with you for a time—if they so choose—by giving you one of their tiny, shimmering scales. Just like with other magical creatures of the wood, however, this must be a gift and not something you pick up without permission, or it won't have any effect and you'll still get colds and flu this winter with the scale in your pocket.

SNAKES

SCIENTIFIC NAME: *Serpentes enchanta*
HABITAT/RANGE: In trees, mainly near water
DIET: Herbivore, love honey and berries
SIZE: The largest recorded was about 6 feet long
ACTIVE TIME: Crepuscular

While these snakes are most active at dusk and dawn, they are also out during the day, though they're probably difficult to spot on any nature walk. They can easily change their shape and color to blend in with their surroundings, becoming little more than another small tree branch or a stick in the mud to avoid detection. Although ordinary snakes are carnivores and unafraid to go after prey, magical snakes are gentle creatures whose favorite treat is lapping honey out of a beehive; their tongues are extra-long and immune to the poison in the bee's stinger. They roam the forest on their own in search of different hives' honey to taste, quickly camouflaging themselves whenever a person or other animal is coming too near. They are especially fearful of magical hedgehogs, who often eat them for dinner.

When they aren't disguising themselves with their magic, however, researchers have observed their true color to be an opaline white—when the sun hits their scales, they shimmer with all the colors of a rainbow. Their scales are also stronger than those of ordinary snakes, more like armor. Somewhere in their history, researchers believe these mild-mannered creatures must have had a common ancestor with dragons, as they can emit small sparks or puffs of smoke when they're overexcited and they have a fringe around their faces they can puff up when they need to look more menacing than they really are.

Should they accidentally slither too far out of the forest, these snakes will still survive; they can adapt quickly to heat or cold, though they prefer to lounge in shady tree branches when they aren't searching for honey or taking a dip in the nearest stream or pond. Though they are still prey to certain magical creatures, their magic makes their scales impossible for humans to pierce. If their skin has been shed freely for humans to pick up, it will grant you protection from bad luck and minor inconveniences, like being late to class or forgetting what you studied the night before for a quiz.

TURTLES

SCIENTIFIC NAME: *Testudines enchanta*
HABITAT/RANGE: In and around water
DIET: Carnivore, especially fish and grindylows
SIZE: Medium, anywhere from 2 feet to 3 feet long
ACTIVE TIME: Diurnal

These turtles, like their ordinary cousins, move rather slowly—
not because they can't shift their legs faster, but because they're
constantly reflecting on things that have already happened as
well as what's going on around them. It can be difficult to spot an
enchanted turtle because quite often researchers have found that
they poke only their head above their favored watery environment,
preferring to stay submerged more often than their ordinary cousins. It's believed they do their best thinking and reflecting while
they're under the surface. However, on the rare occasion that an
enchanted turtle makes their way onto the shore to snack on snails

or smaller fish in the shallows, you'll be treated to a glimpse of their beautiful shells that come in hues of gold and silver and bronze. They're often studded with pearls and other gems, decorated by playful fairies who have had a splash in their waters.

Enchanted turtles are a favorite among other animals of the wood because they like to eat the mean-spirited fairy pests known as grindylows—when they can catch them, which isn't often. They are also a favorite among researchers of magical creatures because their magic allows them to look into the past, and they can help you do the same if you manage to befriend one and encourage it out of the water for a time. One researcher was able to revisit a family memory of a wonderful trip to the beach where she found a shark's tooth while hunting for seashells with her grandfather after sitting with an enchanted turtle for the afternoon.

These turtles are so much larger than ordinary ones because they keep knowledge and secrets stuffed within their shells. These shells grow taller the longer they live, as they stretch with each passing year to hold everything new the turtle has learned and gathered to store there. If you ask nicely, they might share a secret with you as well. You could also whisper a memory or secret of your own to one of these wise creatures for safekeeping.

Amphibians

FROGS

SCIENTIFIC NAME: *Anura enchanta*
HABITAT/RANGE: Ponds and lakes, low-lying wet areas
DIET: Carnivore, love insects and lizards
SIZE: Small, 1 inch up to 6 inches in length
ACTIVE TIME: Diurnal

Although it's widely known that ordinary frogs are nocturnal, enchanted frogs prefer to be most active during the day. If you hear a frog singing and it's only noon, chances are that if you follow the sound (usually a chorus of deep baritones with one or two frogs singing a much higher soprano), you'll find yourself in the presence of a magical creature. These songs are the key to locating them for most researchers; there's more rhythm to their utterances than those of ordinary frogs and more complicated melodies as well. Some sound almost like popular songs you might hear on the radio or online. Once you've discovered the source of this music, approach quietly and with caution and you just might catch a glimpse of these beautiful frogs with their extra-large green eyes and glistening skin. Each one has pale, thin wings on their back that shine with an iridescent rainbow glow in the sunlight; this helps them fly up to gently catch a snack from inside a flower or on a low tree branch that would otherwise be out of their reach.

Enchanted frogs don't sing just for fun, however; they sing to pass on important messages—and not just between the members of their large family groups. They use their deep, or occasionally high, voices to speak with trees and other plants, who they respect like friends and would never consider eating. These frogs have different songs for different purposes, such as singing the plants around them to sleep, soothing plants and trees when they're feeling thirsty or otherwise unwell, and passing along messages from the quiet world of plants to other magical creatures of the wood. Researchers have at times observed the plants taking care of the frogs as well, folding in their petals or leaves to trap a tasty lizard or bug for the frogs to eat.

SALAMANDERS

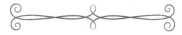

SCIENTIFIC NAME: *Caudata enchanta*
HABITAT/RANGE: Near water
DIET: Carnivore, love bees and dragonflies
SIZE: Extra-small, ½ inch to 2 inches (not including tail)
ACTIVE TIME: Diurnal

Unlike ordinary salamanders, these magical salamanders are most active during daylight hours, so you have a good chance of spotting one even on a quick trip to the woods! Remember, though, they're easily startled, so approach with care or you might blink and find they've already gone, leaving you to wonder if you really saw anything at all. Enchanted salamanders come in a wide array of shimmering pastel colors, and the patterns on their backs are believed to reflect the way the water was rippling at the place and time of their birth. These salamanders are both smaller and lighter weight than ordinary salamanders, and they have incredibly long, curling tails that allow them to hang from the highest tree branches to keep safe while they're sleeping. They also like to hang upside down while catching their meals, and some of their favorite things to eat are enchanted bees and dragonflies, which can almost be as large as them! Their stomachs seem to have no problem expanding to hold big, tasty bugs.

These salamanders are fairly social, so it isn't uncommon to find several in the same tree. While ordinary salamanders hibernate in winter by burying themselves in leaf litter or sinking into the muck at the bottoms of streams, enchanted salamanders curl up in large groups inside the hollows of trees for warmth until spring arrives. Like their more normal cousins, these salamanders have the ability to regrow limbs and organs. However, their magic allows them to do more than that: they can heal physical sickness in other creatures and even humans, helping their bodies to regenerate and recover from illness just as the salamander heals itself. Of course, for their magic to work, they'll have to scurry onto your hand or arm. So once you've found a tree of enchanted salamanders, you'll need to sit and wait patiently in the hopes that one will sense your need and come to you.

TOADS

SCIENTIFIC NAME: *Bufonidae enchanta*
HABITAT/RANGE: Shores of ponds and lakes, wetlands
DIET: Omnivore; flowers, fungi, and snails are some favorites
SIZE: Small, 6 inches long on average
ACTIVE TIME: Diurnal

When you're walking in the woods and pass a mushroom or two, especially a beautiful fly agaric with its bright red top speckled with white dots—the kind of mushrooms that often make up "fairy rings" in popular culture—look a little closer. Does that mushroom appear to be moving slightly? Maybe even breathing? If so, congratulations: you've just stumbled upon an enchanted toad! Most often found near ponds and lakes as children, once they're adults, they can be spotted all over the forest and usually remain in large if scattered groups. Researchers believe that these toads developed their rather confusing and convincing toadstool coloring of red and white on their backs so that they could blend in when people and predators are near, camouflaging themselves to look like ordinary mushrooms and avoid harm. They have small green iridescent wings which aren't always visible, folding into a little chamber in their backs when they aren't in use—although it should be noted that their wings are too small for their bodies and don't actually allow them to fly.

Enchanted toads don't just resemble mushrooms; they also have a taste for true fungi growing in the forest—these are one of their favorite treats. Most of their time, however, isn't spent eating but singing. Much like enchanted frogs, these toads communicate primarily through their songs, which have many purposes. Researchers are constantly taking note of new melodies, and this means it's very likely that each group of toads composes its own songs as well. Their songs are much lower and deeper than those of enchanted frogs, and their melodies are often more like strange chants. One of the most magical things the enchanted toads' songs can do is call down the rain when they're feeling parched or have gotten too far from the water they were born in. If you're ever in the woods and hear a toad singing in the daytime (ordinary toads only croak at night) and notice the sunny sky suddenly turning gray, you might be witnessing a bit of magic. A few have observed that when these toads sing to bring the rain, the little wings on their back flutter in time with the music.

These unusual songs bring good fortune to all other plants and animals who hear them; they can also bring good luck to you.

Birds

CRANES

SCIENTIFIC NAME: *Gruidae enchanta*
HABITAT/RANGE: Near water, lakes or ponds
DIET: Omnivore, fish and cattails
SIZE: Medium, up to 5 feet tall, wingspan up to 8 feet
ACTIVE TIME: Nocturnal

Here are some of the most mysterious animals in the enchanted woods. While they are about the same average height and build as ordinary cranes, they don't come in the usual varied colors that help their nonmagic kin blend in with the wood and wetlands around them. Rather, enchanted cranes are all one solid color—be it white, gray, brown, or black—from the tip of their beak all the way to their feet. These cranes prefer cooler weather and calm conditions. They are almost always found at the water's edge, where they hunt for fish (their favorite meal) and sing mournful songs whose meanings aren't yet clear to researchers. The few observers who have managed to get close enough to a magical crane have each noted that their eyes glow a bright blue when they're singing. Otherwise they are quiet, solitary birds, and you'll never spot two enchanted cranes together. Their family structures are so far entirely a mystery.

Those who have heard these birds have also noticed an effect the song seems to have on them: they've come away from the encounter with a strong new sense of curiosity, particularly about things that are as of yet unknown. One researcher found himself wondering what was at the bottom of the ocean after hearing an enchanted crane, while another started looking up other planets that could possibly support life the way Earth does. Researchers have also noted that the crane's song seems to have the ability to conjure a thick wall of fog even on a sunny day, giving the crane some privacy and the cool, overcast conditions that they prefer. Those who have gotten a little too close while caught up in their studies have also learned that these cranes can use their feet to make rather frightening shadow puppets in the mist to scare people away when they feel threatened.

EAGLES

SCIENTIFIC NAME: *Accipitridae enchanta*
HABITAT/RANGE: Mountain peaks, treetops
DIET: Carnivore, fish and amphibians
SIZE: Extra-large, up to 60 inches tall, wingspan up to 12 feet
ACTIVE TIME: Diurnal

Meet the most powerful predators of the enchanted skies. With the largest wingspans and sharpest eyes of any bird in the magical woods, these giant eagles go where they want, when they want, and befriend only those who prove themselves truly worthy of their trust and respect. Roughly the size of large dogs when their wings are folded in, these eagles either like to keep to the treetops for privacy reasons or they are simply few in number, as they aren't often seen even within the enchanted wood—but when they are, there's no mistaking them, as they fly higher than any other birds' wings will carry them. Their sharp eyes are a deep amber in color, while their feathers come in colors like copper, silver, gold, bronze, and rose gold. Fairies have been known to collect enchanted eagles' naturally shed feathers to use in their clothing, like decorating dresses or making crowns—though even they have to be careful, as these feathers are sharp rather than soft.

These eagles all have perfect vision, as it's their eyesight that holds their magic: as they soar up high, they can see everything clearly—past, present, and future. There have only been two instances of researchers managing to speak to one of these amazing and intimidating birds. In both cases, after the person shared what was on their mind, the eagle was able to offer excellent advice about how to move forward with whatever was troubling them.

There's a chance you can befriend one of these eagles for yourself, but only if you give them plenty of space to approach you on their own terms. And remember, don't ask them for a ride on their back: while they're certainly big and strong enough to carry you, they will only allow sick or injured animals to ride on their backs—although rumor has it they have occasionally offered rides to lost or stranded travelers as well.

GOSHAWKS

SCIENTIFIC NAME: *Buteo enchanta*
HABITAT/RANGE: Treetops, mountain peaks, and skies
DIET: Carnivore, eat small fairies and anything they catch
SIZE: Medium, about 3 feet long, wingspan up to 6 feet
ACTIVE TIME: Diurnal

These stunning birds come in a wide array of colors you won't see in ordinary hawks—like soft white, deep earthy green, and even deep indigo. The patterns of their feathers reflect the landscape of the magical woods in which they hatched. Much larger than ordinary hawks, enchanted hawk parents often have to build their nests in small caves or rocky outcroppings that can support the weight of the large silver and gold eggs from which these hawk babies hatch. Enchanted hawks are experts at hiding their nests to protect them from predators, so if you want to see one of these amazing birds, your best bet is searching the treetops or sky. While they may be larger than their ordinary cousins, these hawks are equally incredible fliers and known among the other enchanted creatures of the wood as experts in flight. In fact, if you spot one of them in the air, chances are they're doing tricks midflight to impress their friends.

All day long, no matter the weather, they race and dive from sky to trees searching for small tasty fairies and other enchanted creatures to eat, diving at speeds of up to 200 miles per hour while on the hunt. They seem to have developed a taste for magic in their meals; researchers are currently investigating whether a steady diet of fairies and other enchanted creatures strengthens their own magic.

These hawks don't sing; they whistle. And this is how they access their magic, which allows them to control the wind. It took researchers many years of observation to realize that the reason these hawks can fly in any weather is because their unique whistles change the wind in their favor even during a storm. If you catch one of their feathers out of the air and imitate their whistle, the wind will change for you, too.

OWLS

SCIENTIFIC NAME: *Strigiformes enchanta*
HABITAT/RANGE: Trees overlooking meadows, warm or cold
DIET: Carnivore, love lizards and rodents
SIZE: Extra-small to medium, wingspan up to 8 feet
ACTIVE TIME: Diurnal

Like other owls, enchanted owls vary greatly in size: they can be as big as a toddler with a wingspan stretching an impressive eight feet, soaring up in the sky and competing with the giant enchanted eagles for food, or they can be as small as your pinkie finger and nearly impossible to spot as they hop from branch to branch chasing bugs. A gathering of ordinary owls is known as a *parliament*, but enchanted owls refer to their own frequent scholarly gatherings as a *council*, where they get together to have deep discussions and learn new things. The history of fairies is one of their favorite subjects. Other than through their size, you'll know you're in the presence of an enchanted owl because their feathers shimmer as though they've been dusted with glitter and they leave a little sparkle behind whenever they depart from their latest perch.

Traditionally, ordinary owls have long been symbols of wisdom, and magic owls are also very wise. They value clear communication above all else, whether through song, a poem or story read aloud, or simply good conversation that makes them think. Because of this, enchanted owls have become highly skilled at learning many different languages. They can screech like an eagle, sing sweetly with the sparrows, whisper to the wind, or even call out to lost hikers to try to get them back on the right path—without glancing up into the trees, it would be easy to mistake their speaking voices for another human. One sure way to draw an enchanted owl to you is to tell some stories or read aloud. And while ordinary owls are nocturnal, enchanted owls are mostly active during the day because that's when their favorite lizards and other prey are easiest to find, so you can rest assured they'll be awake to hear you.

If an enchanted owl offers you one of its feathers, take it! This magical gift will allow you the ability to speak with animals—magic and nonmagic alike—for the day, just like the enchanted owls can.

SPARROWS

SCIENTIFIC NAME: *Passeridae enchanta*
HABITAT/RANGE: Lower tree branches, forest floor
DIET: Herbivore, prefer seeds and nuts, flower nectar
SIZE: Extra-small, up to 1 inch
ACTIVE TIME: Diurnal

One of the most social birds in the magical wood, these sparrows live, travel, and play in groups known as *celebrations*. While ordinary sparrows can grow up to about six inches or more in length, enchanted sparrows are much smaller: only about the size of moths. Blink and you'll miss them. However, if you do spot one, it's likely thanks to their vivid colors—the undersides of their feathers come in a wide variety of neon hues, with rainbow being the most common. Aside from their bright coloring and tiny size, they look just like ordinary sparrows, and they eat many of the same things— seeds and nuts are some of their favorites. So if you're minding your steps while out in the woods, you might be able to spot several of these little creatures hopping along the ground in search of their next meal.

Down on the forest floor, they also gather anything that catches their eye, from shiny trash left behind by campers and day hikers to flowers with petals as bright as their feathers. They take their prizes to the lower branches of trees (about as high as their tiny wings can carry them) to use as material for their nests.

While these sparrows may be challenging to see, you can certainly hear them on your next forest adventure if you know what to listen for: a soft, cheerful tune that makes you want to dance. Even fairies aren't immune to their catchy melodies and will often dance in fairy rings because they've heard the sparrows. These sweet birds always have a reason to sing, because they're always happy, always together, and always having fun with each other as they make music and search for their favorite treats or build their shiny nests. Their magic is in their song, too. If you listen long enough, these sparrows can help you remember things you've forgotten, from the important to the small—from the chore you were supposed to do last night or a joke you've been wanting to tell to things like precious early memories and long-ago childhood friends.

WOODPECKERS

SCIENTIFIC NAME: *Picidae enchanta*
HABITAT/RANGE: Anywhere within the trees
DIET: Omnivore, enjoy nectar, berries, and bugs
SIZE: Small, about 18 inches tall, wingspan up to 30 inches
ACTIVE TIME: Diurnal

These woodpeckers may look almost like ordinary ones until you get up close, but then you'll notice the deep amber of their eyes. Their feathers are a mix of white, brown, and black, as might be expected, but watching these enchanted birds over time will reveal how their feathers change color as they communicate with the tree they've chosen to guard, shifting to reflect the tree's mood and needs. Researchers are beginning to work out what the different hues mean: all white feathers signal a tree in need of water, while deep green feathers mean the tree is perfectly content, and brown feathers indicate the tree needs more nutrients to keep growing. An enchanted woodpecker is most often drawn to a dead or dying tree, just like their ordinary cousins, though not for the same reasons; enchanted woodpeckers know that these trees are in need of greater care and want to help. They usually bond with a tree and become its caretaker for life. And while more fieldwork is needed on their selection process, researchers have been able to visit a certain woodpecker at the same oak tree every week, another at a leaning birch tree, and so on.

When an enchanted woodpecker takes care of a specific tree, that tree also provides for them, giving off a wonderful scent to draw bugs near for the birds to catch and eat. The trees will also run with sweet sap for the woodpecker to drink. Enchanted woodpeckers communicate with their tree through tapping. Their beaks hold magic that can turn a pocket of the tree hollow and allow them to store things inside, like the beautiful gemstone-colored eggs they lay. Those eggs are considered a delicacy among fairies for dinners and feast days, so being able to hide them in a safe place ensures the magical woodpecker's survival. As far as researchers can tell, the trees don't mind participating in this part of the process because they're so well taken care of. If you show respect to the trees and ask one of these woodpeckers nicely, they just might store an item you need to keep hidden as well.

Fish

. . . .

CATFISH

SCIENTIFIC NAME: *Siluriformes enchanta*

HABITAT/RANGE: Lakes and ponds

DIET: Omnivore, prefer algae and plants, sometimes fruit

SIZE: Small, up to 20 inches

ACTIVE TIME: Crepuscular

If you're out sitting on the shore of a lake or pond and suddenly feel a deep calm wash over you no matter what's on your mind, you just might be in the presence of an enchanted catfish. While there are many types of ordinary catfish and their features vary greatly, enchanted catfish are one species and have much in common even if their appearances and sizes can vary slightly from fish to fish. Researchers learned early into their observations that the whiskers of these fish change color with their mood, shifting from light to dark. They are also covered in a hard outer shell that resembles armor rather than scales, protecting their soft insides. The color of their armor can be gray, brown, or off-white, or more commonly a combination of white with colored spots that researchers like to call *calico*. Enchanted catfish most often emerge from the lake bottom to swim and search for food around dawn and dusk. They aren't shy and will happily come up to the lakeshore in groups as long as they're still partially submerged, snacking on weeds and hoping that a friendly hand will reach down to rub their heads and whiskers (they especially love being rubbed behind the ears) while they eat and bask in the soft light.

Enchanted catfish have moments of documented playfulness, but they are most often calm—a state that turns their whiskers a soft brown. Perhaps this is because their favorite thing to do underwater is snuggle with each other like a pile of ordinary cats, which they more closely resemble in personality than any sort of fish. Their magic allows them to calm the emotions of others simply by being near them, and they bring a loving, healing energy to anyone who is lucky enough to encounter them. Putting your hand out to carefully pet an enchanted catfish—with an adult's supervision, of course—can help you feel balanced and peaceful for the rest of the day.

LARGEMOUTH BASS

SCIENTIFIC NAME: *Micropterus enchanta*
HABITAT/RANGE: Murky, deep waters
DIET: Carnivore, small fish and false fireflies
SIZE: Medium, up to 40 inches
ACTIVE TIME: Crepuscular

Although sightings of these enchanted fish are rare, dawn and dusk are the best times to have even a chance of spotting these magical bass hunting for fairies known as false fireflies to spit out of the sky. (These bass hunt their prey by spitting to stun them.) In fact, hunting is the only occasion when these enchanted fish slither up from the murky bottoms of lakes where they spend most of their time with no pesky currents to disturb their rest. These fish are instantly recognizable as different from their more ordinary cousins by their larger size, incredibly slow movements, and distinct looks: they have gemstone-colored scales and moon-white eyes that seem to glow with some secret magic.

What that secret is, researchers have yet to determine, but they suspect it has to do with moving through life with deliberate slowness. These enchanted bass operate so slowly that it takes them a year to eat just a single meal once they finally catch something—be it fairy or fish—and luckily that's enough to sustain them. When they aren't busy sleeping and digesting, they love rolling in cool, slippery mud that coats their scales and seems to prevent aging.

Researchers first discovered magical bass and their ability to slow down time when having a picnic on the shore of a small lake. One woman finished her lunch and decided to camp there for the afternoon, reading an entire book over several hours before rejoining her group—only to find once she left the pond that, for her friends, barely a few minutes had gone by since they last saw her and finished their meal. Enchanted bass remind us to take it easy and that time taken to move slowly, with intention, is time well spent.

SALMON

SCIENTIFIC NAME: *Salmo enchanta*
HABITAT/RANGE: Fast-moving rivers and streams
DIET: Carnivore, prefer worms and other smaller fish
SIZE: Medium, up to 60 inches
ACTIVE TIME: Diurnal

At first glance, these magical fish appear to have light gray bodies
dappled with darker spots and a splash of pink or white on their
bellies, much like ordinary salmon. However, enchanted salmon
are much larger—sometimes double the length and weight of their
ordinary cousins—and in direct sunlight, the true glittering rainbow of their scales is revealed. These salmon seem to have become
larger and larger over time, and research suggests the reason they've
evolved this way is because enchanted chipmunks and certain fairies have become fond of riding on their backs as a means to explore
a wider area of the forest, cruising up and down rivers and streams
to their destinations or sometimes even for the thrill of it, asking

the salmon to put on some extra speed. Their quick nature is also a survival skill: enchanted otters and eagles are especially fond of making these salmon into their dinner. Enchanted turtles often dream of dining on one of these huge, juicy salmon, but they've never been quick enough to catch one.

Thanks to their speed, these pack-swimming salmon are always able to eat their fill, even during leaner seasons like winter; rather than rest down in the muddy river bottom, they continue to search for tasty worms and small fish. Researchers suspect that because they're so well-fed and plump, the cold doesn't really bother them. Enchanted salmon seem to know that in order to play and swim and explore their hardest, they need to eat well and take care of their physical and mental health. This is why they always seem so cheerful when they leap from the river to put on a show for whoever happens to be nearby. If you go fishing with the hope of catching one of these salmon, you won't get more than a huge dinner; however, if you sit quietly by the riverbank and let the enchanted salmon approach you, they just might share one of their scales with you. This sparkling treasure will gift you their wisdom and inspire you to take excellent care of yourself all year round.

SUNFISH

SCIENTIFIC NAME: *Lepomis enchanta*
HABITAT/RANGE: Warm, slow-moving water
DIET: Omnivore, favor small fish, sun sylphs, and plant matter
SIZE: Small, up to 20 inches long
ACTIVE TIME: Diurnal

Your best chance of spotting an enchanted sunfish is to go to the woods on the warmest day and find the hottest, most sluggish pool of water. These fish don't like currents, which interfere with their peaceful floating and sunbathing. They always stay in areas of water where the sunlight touches except when they need to dive for a bite to eat, so there's no need to go fishing just in the hope of finding one of these dazzling creatures. Unlike ordinary freshwater sunfish, which come in an array of beautiful colors themselves, enchanted sunfish all glow with a bit of actual sunlight trapped beneath their scales; in fact, they might have some color, but no researcher can say because they're so bright to look at that humans are always forced to turn away. Glancing at one for too long can leave you seeing spots, as more than one researcher has learned the hard way. When they swim or sunbathe in schools—as they mostly prefer to do—they appear as sunbeams dappling the surface of the water.

Like the sun from which these fish take their name, enchanted sunfish have a cheerful disposition at all times. They're never in a bad mood because they have so much to be grateful for, according to a researcher who had some help in translating a conversation with one of these bright creatures. They're thankful for the warmth of the water on their scales and for their beautiful surroundings, as well as any who come to visit them. They deeply appreciate the little things in life, like their tasty meals of smaller fish, bits of plants, and whatever else the wind might blow their way.

If you find them, enchanted sunfish can help you remember the best day of your life; you may not be able to look directly at the fish themselves, but they'll replay your fondest memories reflected in the surface of their watery home.

TROUT

SCIENTIFIC NAME: *Irideus enchanta*
HABITAT/RANGE: Deep, murky pools and ponds
DIET: Carnivore, prefer insects, small fish,
snails, bubble sprites
SIZE: Medium, up to 50 inches long
ACTIVE TIME: Nocturnal

Some researchers have spent their whole lives hoping for a glimpse of a magical trout, searching in every pond they can find in the wood only to come up empty-handed: these enchanted fish are quite rare. They prefer to live in large, very deep pools where they can swim and occasionally sunbathe in peace, although they do most of their eating and working by night. Enchanted trout have wonderfully creative minds, which they most often put to use constructing homes underwater. They make entire castles from the bubbles they blow or else shape them out of the thick, muddy sand at the bottom of their pool. They then decorate these homes with whatever they can find. These trout are bigger and longer than their ordinary cousins (who only grow to a length of about thirty inches) and have brighter, almost neon pink bellies. The pink coloring extends up into their sides, too. Some have dark speckles that seem to glimmer when exposed to sunlight. The long whiskers of these trout indicate their age, and some drag the very bottom of the deep pools where they live, as enchanted trout can actually live forever if they don't become a magical crane or eagle's dinner.

Because magical trout are so old and wise, they prefer to be addressed as Grandmother or Grandfather. This is important to keep in mind when speaking to them, because they can grant you a single wish if you approach with respect and talk to them politely. If English isn't your first language and you don't speak Trout, don't worry; these fish are very intelligent and are born with the magical gift of being able to speak any language.

It is most important to consider what you'll wish for if you manage to find an enchanted trout, researchers caution—your wish will indeed come true, but wishes often turn out differently than the person making them believes they should.

Arthropods

· · · · · · · · · · · · ·

BEES

SCIENTIFIC NAME: *Anthophila enchanta*
HABITAT/RANGE: Hives are in trees; often seen in meadows
DIET: Herbivore, love nectar, pollen, and overripe fruit
SIZE: Small, 1 inch long at most
ACTIVE TIME: Diurnal

Ordinary bees buzz, but enchanted bees sing. So following some unusual music in the wood is one way you might stumble across a hive of these magical hard workers. Bees are known for being very noisy because their wings beat so fast (11,400 times in one minute), but these enchanted bees' wings produce a pleasant whistling sound that accompanies their song. By appearance, they're a little smaller than an ordinary bumblebee, making them a good size for carefully perching on herbs and flowers and other growing things. Unlike their ordinary cousins, their wings glitter in the sun and the hair on their bodies is more like fur. If you get close enough to pet one, you'll find it's silky soft to the touch. (It's important to note that enchanted bees only like to be touched carefully, with one finger petting their backs.)

Bees—both magic and nonmagic alike—communicate through a series of dance moves, although enchanted bees also rely on their songs to tell each other where they're heading next. Just like their ordinary cousins, these bees are also cheerful and hardworking, flying from flower to flower from sunup to sundown to make the most of every waking moment. Researchers have observed that these bees have the ability to heal plants: when the bees sing to them, it seems to help struggling plants and flowers find the sun. They also feed any sick or dying plants with their enchanted honey to give them strength. Their honey is said to taste like a dark vanilla with a touch of lavender.

If you do happen upon an enchanted bee while in the woods, don't worry: they don't sting unless you're hurting their plants by ripping them out of the ground or plucking the heads off their flowers, in which case they'll leave a nasty mark to let others know you're not a friend of the forest. The mark, much to the relief of one researcher who was in the wood to study magical plants, does eventually come off with soap and water.

BEETLES

SCIENTIFIC NAME: *Coleoptera enchanta*
HABITAT/RANGE: Under logs, rocks, leaf litter on forest floor
DIET: Omnivore, consume other insects and plants
SIZE: Extra-small, half an inch to 1 inch in length
ACTIVE TIME: Diurnal

These tiny beetles are small but powerful, and they are one of the hardest enchanted creatures in the wood to spot. Even during daylight, they prefer spending their time hiding under logs or leaf litter on the forest floor. If you're lucky enough to turn over a rock and uncover one— or several, as they tend to stay in family groups— you'll find that, up close, their carapaces are rainbow-colored and iridescent when the sunlight hits them. Constantly in motion and busy foraging for dead insects or plants—these beetles never hunt for a meal and eat only what they can find already dead—they scurry close to the ground on their little legs where they can feel every motion of the earth beneath them. They can fly, although only for a few inches at a time and not very high in the air—nor would they want to leave the ground so far behind. Their wings seem to be a trait left over from some distant ancestor. But like enchanted butterflies, a certain shimmering dust coats these wings; perhaps that is a clue to their heritage.

Another challenge to spotting these small, enchanted beetles is their ability to camouflage themselves; they can change color completely, becoming as dark as the rock they're under or as unremarkable as the log they're hiding in. They can turn leaf green or start to resemble the petals of any number of flowers when they're trying to blend in with their surroundings. Researchers also wonder if perhaps they take on the color of any plant they decide they like, not just disguising themselves in moments when they're trying to hide. Being so connected to the Earth and all who share it, these beetles do have magic they can offer you, as one researcher discovered quite by accident while wiping sweat from her eyes after touching one of these magical beetles: the shimmering dust from their backs, if sprinkled into your eyes, gives you the ability to see fairies for about a full day.

BUTTERFLIES

SCIENTIFIC NAME: *Rhopalocera enchanta*
HABITAT/RANGE: Flowering bushes, meadows
DIET: Herbivore, love herbs, flowers, nectar
SIZE: Extra-small to small, wingspan ranges
from 1 inch to 10 inches
ACTIVE TIME: Diurnal

These butterflies—whether they're as tiny as part of your finger or as big as the spread of your entire hand—are always coasting from one plant to the next on their shimmering wings. Look closely at the next butterfly you see in the woods, and if glitter appears to fall from their wings when they take flight, you'll know you've found an enchanted butterfly. Some researchers in the past mistook these graceful creatures for fairies because they're so colorful even along their bodies—and some fairies with similar wings also have antennae, to make matters more confusing. These butterflies' wing colors and patterns vary as much as their size; however, the patterns on their wings are far different from those of ordinary butterflies. A close observer—or one with great binoculars hiding in some nearby bushes to do some butterfly-watching—might notice that rather than forming random shapes or curves, the dark swirls on their otherwise brightly hued wings are bits of writing: words from letters that people left unsent or ones that were otherwise lost before the recipient had a chance to read them.

One way to know that you've found an enchanted butterfly rather than a fairy is the way they move: they fly more slowly even than ordinary butterflies, coasting on each little breeze and letting the wind blow their antennae back from their heads in moments of pure joy. These butterflies embody peace and calm, taking their time to notice everything about their surroundings while they sip the most fragrant nectars and herbs from plants growing in the wood.

If an enchanted butterfly lands on you, their magic allows them to heal sadness, helping make bad memories and thoughts less painful for a time. People who have encountered one of these magical butterflies report feeling more at peace with their problems and sorrows after visiting with them even for a short time.

DRAGONFLIES

SCIENTIFIC NAME: *Anisoptera enchanta*
HABITAT/RANGE: Near water
DIET: Carnivore, eat only dead things
SIZE: Small, 2–6 inches in length, wingspan up to 2 feet
ACTIVE TIME: Diurnal

If you're near a lake or pond, especially one where there are few or no other people around, keep an eye out for these water-loving magical insects. Unlike ordinary dragonflies, these creatures can both fly over low distances and swim in shallow water, which they are known to love. They are somewhat larger than ordinary dragon-flies, and their wings are so big that they more closely resemble fossils of dragonflies that go back millions of years. Their wingspan can grow up to two feet wide, and a close look will reveal patterns of little sunrays on their wings. Researchers suspect they grow so large because there are higher levels of oxygen and nutrients in magical woods. Their bodies are often iridescent shades of red, orange, and yellow, or a blend of all three. With such bright colors, they're known to inspire hope in anyone who happens to spot them. They have the same sharp teeth as their ordinary cousins, but these dragonflies don't bite or catch and eat live bugs—in fact, they don't eat anything living. Other animals of the wood recognize the important role they play in the forest ecosystem by eating only things that have died.

Enchanted dragonflies love to hum and sing. They travel in small groups, composing their own songs as they go about their days, often joining each other for a chorus. So keeping your ears open is another way you can try to locate these amazing creatures. They're exactly who you want to find on an overcast day when you had hoped to go swimming: their magic is in their ability to conjure sunbeams with a flap of their wings, which is powerful enough to draw rays of sun through the thickest clouds and down into what-ever area of the wood they happen to be buzzing around in.

MOTHS

SCIENTIFIC NAME: *Heterocera enchanta*
HABITAT/RANGE: Most often seen in moonlit meadows
DIET: Herbivore, fruit and flowers
SIZE: Small, wingspan up to 5 inches
ACTIVE TIME: Nocturnal

Emerging from their rest as the moon rises, enchanted moths most closely resemble the ordinary insect known as a rosy maple moth. These stunning yellow and pink moths are larger, however, with a wingspan of about five inches. (The largest magical moth a researcher has recorded had a wingspan of six inches.) Also their bodies seem to glow from within as if they each hold a bit of moonlight—which researchers suspect they might. You'll often find these luminous beauties in the quietest meadows when the moon is waxing—getting larger—or full; they have never been seen on the night of a new moon, when there doesn't appear to be a moon in the sky at all. Often hungry, these moths gently flutter on top of whatever flower or fruit has lured them close to take a bite, and as they flap their wings, you can determine if you are in the presence of an enchanted moth by looking closely at the colorful body underneath. Their bodies are covered in long, silky hair that shines a bright white.

These moths are known among the magical wood for noticing things that others don't, like an injured creature hiding in the shadows. Researchers suspect this is thanks to all the extra moonlight that they conjure with their magic. Where enchanted dragonflies are able to call forth sunbeams with a flap of their wings, enchanted moths draw down moonbeams even on cloudy nights by flapping their wings as they fly. If enough of them are together in one area, they can fully draw out the moon from behind the clouds, as one researcher was lucky enough to witness. These enchanted moths dance and play all night, cartwheeling midair in the moonlight while whispering overheard secrets to each other and passing private messages among the other creatures of the magical woods.

SPIDERS

SCIENTIFIC NAME: *Araneae enchanta*
HABITAT/RANGE: Dark, shadowy places, especially dense trees
DIET: Carnivore, eat any insect or fairy caught in their webs
SIZE: Extra-small: the largest recorded was less than half an inch
ACTIVE TIME: Crepuscular

If you want to spot an enchanted spider, you're really going to need a sense of adventure, as you'll have to get deep into the trees to the places where branches all tangle together and it's difficult to find a way forward; this is where magical spiders like to spin their webs, as they're kept safe from other creatures, humans, and fairies by the dense growth. You're most likely to see one of their enormous webs before you see them—if you ever do, thanks to their extremely small size. However, once you've found a web and you're looking closely, their bright colors set them apart from ordinary spiders. Their compact, rather furry bodies come in hues from purple to cotton candy pink to neon yellow. While ordinary spiders have eight eyes, these magical spiders have up to twelve, which allows them to look in many different places at once—not just all around them, above and below, but also into the past and far into the future.

Even if you don't see the enchanted spider, but only their web, this alone is well worth a look. Their webs are like mirrors, full of symbols and spells that allow them to take a closer look at things that haven't yet happened but could. These highly intelligent spiders pride themselves on their structure and organization and are some of the finest architects in the magical wood. Be careful getting too close to one of these huge webs (they can stretch over seven feet in any direction), as they're incredibly sticky—and also take the enchanted spiders a lot of work to create, so it would be a shame to destroy one. But if you do touch one by mistake, you'll be able to tell them apart from ordinary spiderwebs by licking the residue from your hand; enchanted spiderwebs taste like spun sugar, and in fact, researchers have confirmed this is what they're made of. If you manage to find an enchanted spider at work and ask nicely, they might let you take a look into their web so you can see some of your potential future.

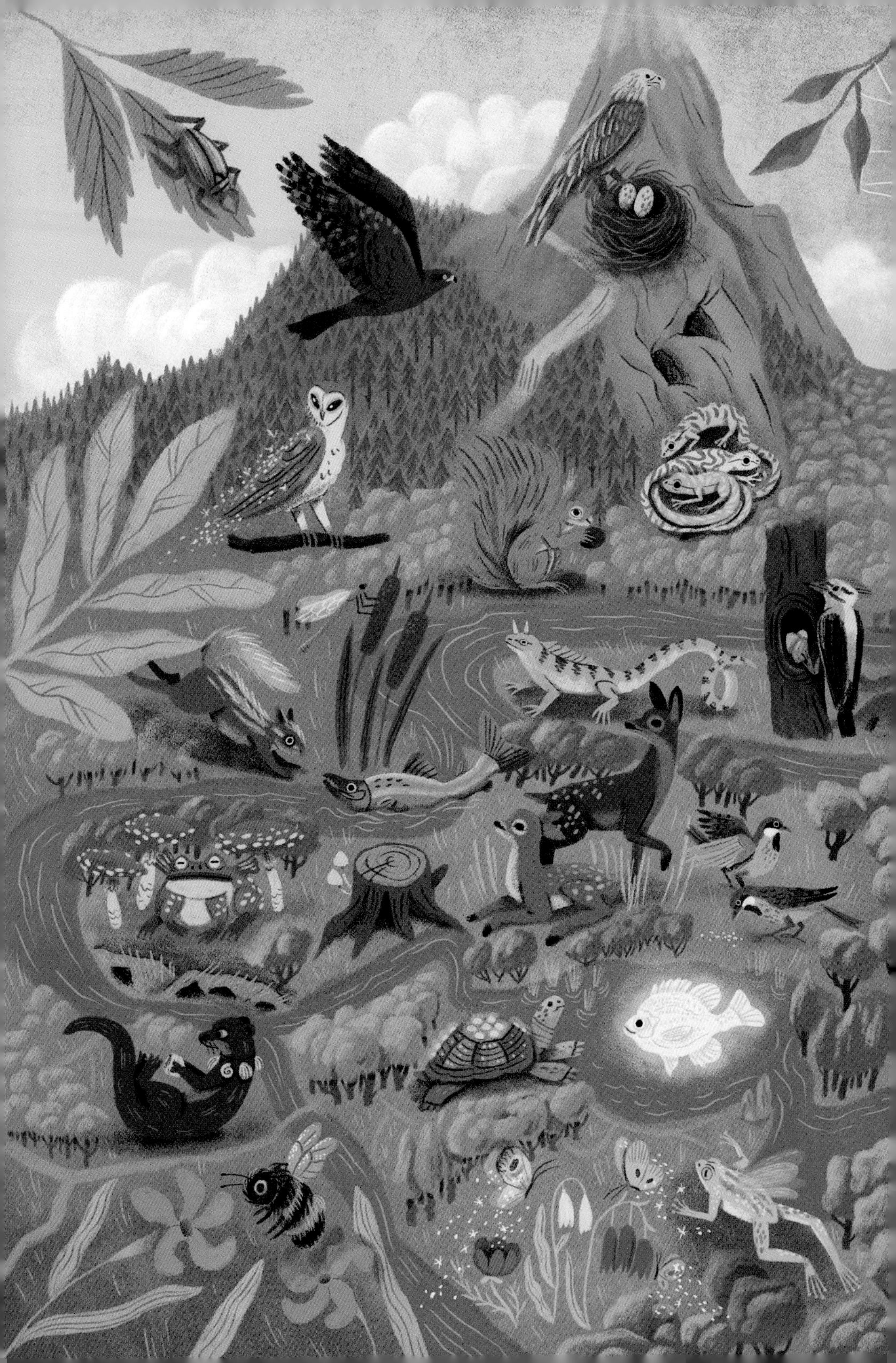

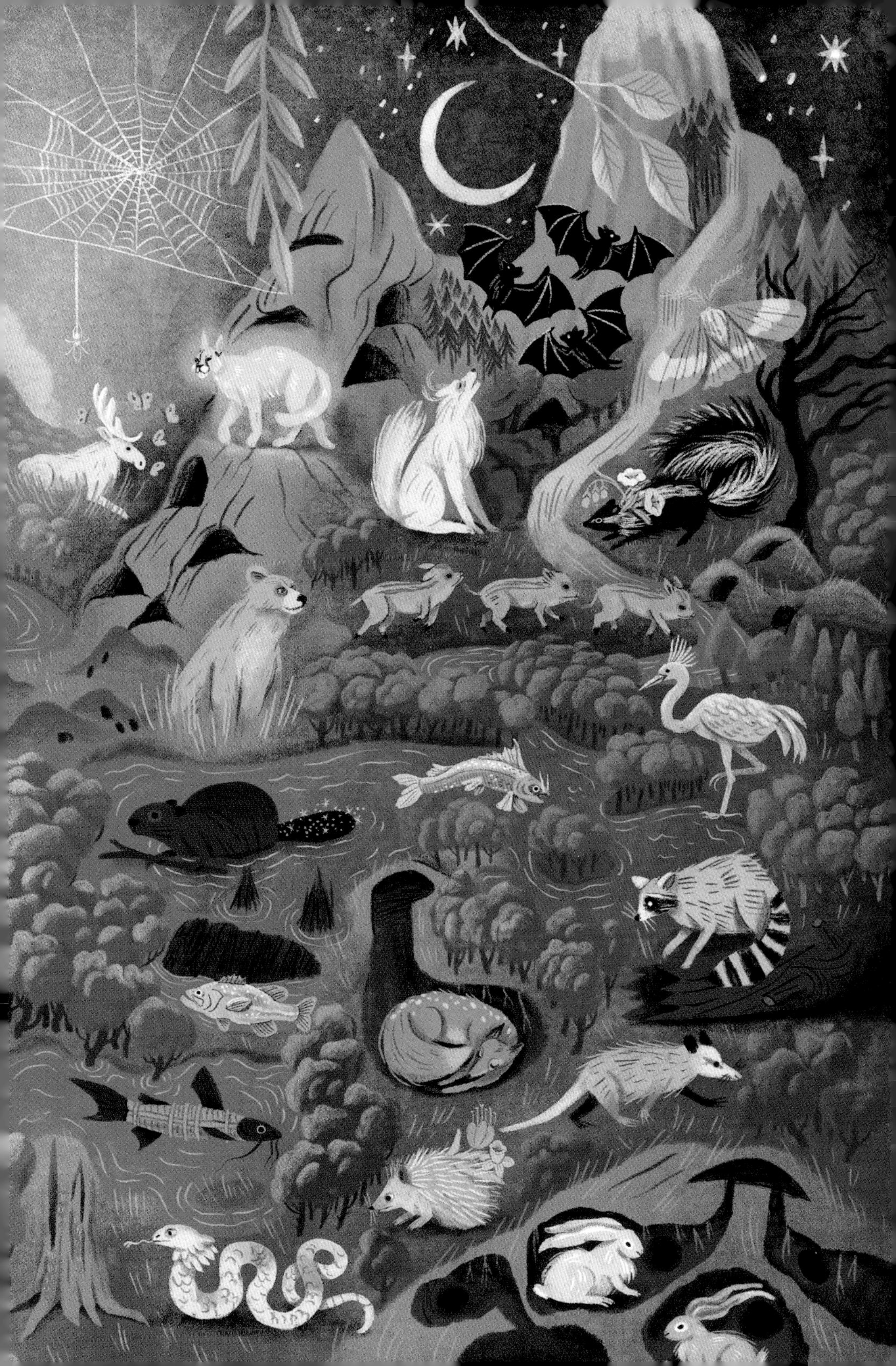

When you
make your
path forward,
even if you don't
know the way,
that's where the
magic happens.

MAGICAL
ACTIVITIES
AND QUIZZES

On the following pages, you'll find some ways you can bring a bit of the enchanted woodlands into your daily life—whether by making treats and shelters for the creatures of the woods, creating leaf prints from some of the animals' favorite trees, learning how to identify certain tracks and pawprints, or packing a bag for a day hike into the woods to maybe discover some of these amazing creatures for yourself.

There are also quizzes to help you determine which woodland creature type best fits with your personality—and even what kind of hidden magical power you would have if you lived in the enchanted wood.

Have fun making some magic!

LEAF PRINTING 101

While it is best practices to leave most of what you find in the woods—even things that are on the ground might be used by certain animals as materials for a home or a nest—collecting some fallen leaves from animals' favorite trees like birch, elm, and yew can be a terrific way to remember your magical time out in the wild. Here is a way to take the leaves you collect on your adventures and turn them into something as bright and magical as the creatures themselves.

Materials Needed

- Real fallen leaves, fresh or dry
- Outdoor workspace or newspaper to put down (This can get messy!)
- Paper, fabric, or canvas board
- A colorful assortment of paints (acrylic paint if using fabric; many types of paint will work on paper or canvas board)
- Paper plate or other paint palette
- Paintbrushes

Directions

1. To find your leaves, go into the woods and collect some! See if you can get a few from each of the magical creatures' favorite trees as outlined in the Herbarium earlier in this book.

2. Get your work area ready: either choose a safe area outside where an adult won't mind some messy paint or lay down newspapers or a mat you can get paint on where you'll be working. Make sure you have your canvas, paper, or piece of fabric ready and that it's the size you want. Otherwise, ask an adult for help cutting it to the right size. Put the different colors of paint you'd like to use—the more, the better—on a paper plate.

3. Paint a leaf! Choose your first leaf and flip it over so the underside is facing you. Cover it in the paint color of your choice.

4. Place the leaf with the painted side down against your paper or fabric. Press down all over the leaf for several seconds to make sure the paint transfers onto your canvas or paper.

5. Lift the leaf away to reveal your colorful print.

6. Repeat steps 3–5 with as many different leaves as you can fit into your paper or canvas.

7. Give the paint time to dry, then enjoy your reminder of the enchanted wood!

TRIM A "TREAT TREE"
FOR WOODLAND CREATURES

When we go visit someone's house, it can be nice to bring something with us. Often we bring cookies or another treat to share. Maybe the next time you go into the woods, you'd like to make some safe treats that can be enjoyed by magic and nonmagical creatures alike. Here is one suggestion for doing just that: a treat tree, which can be enjoyed by the animals of the wood, especially birds, at any time of year.

Materials Needed

- Unseasoned popcorn, popped
- Cranberries
- Twine
- Needle and thread (with adult supervision, optional)
- Wax paper
- Molasses
- Wild birdseed mix (ask a local pet store for the best choice)
- A bowl
- Fresh apples

(Materials continue on next page.)

- Cardboard, stencils, and scissors (optional)
- Peanut butter
- Honey
- Seeds (such as pumpkin or sunflower seeds)
- Breadcrumbs
- Dried corn kernels

Directions

1. Choose a tree near the edge of the woods in an open field as the place you'll hang your treats—one that has plenty of branches you can reach. If you feel unsure, ask an adult for help confirming your choice.

2. Make your treats a day or two before you plan to decorate your treat tree, if you like. Store them in a dry container or baggies to keep them fresh.

3. Get your work area ready: either choose a safe area outside where an adult won't mind some mess, or lay down newspapers or a mat on the place where you'll be working.

4. The first treat you could consider making is popcorn garlands. Set out your popcorn and cranberries. Then using a large needle—and with an adult's help or supervision— thread them onto a length of sewing thread that can be wrapped around a branch. Have fun alternating or making patterns with the two materials.

5. The next treat you could make are garlands of birdseed and molasses to wrap around branches. Put some molasses in a bowl, then dip a long piece of twine in it. Next dip the sticky twine into some birdseed. These treats could be layered between wax paper to prevent them from sticking to each other.

6. Whole fresh apples can be tied to a branch using your twine; wrap one end of the twine tightly around the fruit's stem and knot it, and then secure the other end to a branch. Alternatively, you could core your apple, cut thick slices, and use your twine to hang those. Or you could core your apple and loop the twine through the hole.

7. You can also make your own shaped treat ornaments using cardboard and scissors. You may want stencils to trace certain shapes like circles or stars onto your cardboard before cutting them out. Put a small hole in the top of your shape, just large enough to loop some twine through for hanging. Cover both sides of your cardboard shape in a layer of peanut butter, honey, or molasses, or some mixture of all three. Then sprinkle seeds (pumpkin seeds, sunflower seeds, wild birdseed are all good ideas), breadcrumbs, and dried corn kernels onto the sticky mixture on each side. Wax paper could be used to help keep these treats from sticking to each other.

8. Don't forget to make a mix for creatures who can't fly as well! Combine leftover birdseed with breadcrumbs and dried corn kernels and store in a container or baggie.

9. Decorate your tree! Take an adult with you in case you need help reaching certain branches. Once your treats are hung, scatter your mixture for the ground-dwelling creatures before you leave. The creatures of the wood will surely appreciate your visit!

BUILD A SHELTER FOR WOODLAND CREATURES

Everyone likes a little shelter from a storm, and the magical creatures of the wood are no exception! Sometimes, for whatever reason, a creature may find themselves far from home when a storm arrives and will have to search for some cover close by. You can help them out by making a temporary safe space for them. Some animals may even use the shelter you make as a place to hibernate during the winter or as a nest in which to have their young. The type of shelter we're going to describe how to build here is often called a *hedgehog house*.

For this activity, you'll need a trusted adult to help with some of the work! Hopefully they will also love animals like you do.

Materials Needed

- Large cardboard box
- Knife (for your adult to use)

(Materials continue on next page.)

- Twigs
- Dry leaves (for decoration and/or for bedding)
- Art supplies to decorate the house: paint, crayons, markers
- Straw or shredded paper (for bedding)

Directions

1. Get your trusted adult and your materials together in a good workspace, ideally outdoors.
2. Have your adult use the knife to cut a circular entryway of about five inches around into your box. This is how creatures will come and go.
3. Optional: Create a small tunnel using another piece of cardboard and attach it to the entrance to your hedgehog house. This will prevent predators from being able to stick a paw inside and will keep any small creatures using your shelter even safer.
4. Have your adult help you cut some small air vents into the side of the house. Everyone needs fresh air!
5. Now comes the fun part: decorating the house! Magical woodland creatures appreciate a well-decorated house as much as the next person. Twigs and dry leaves are great choices for decorations and will help the shelter feel like it's truly part of the wood. You can also use markers and crayons, preferably in colors you'd find in the forest, to add some pretty art to the shelter.
6. Next, we need to make a cozy place for creatures to sleep inside. A layer of dry leaves, shredded paper, or straw will do

nicely. Some favorite nesting leaves of smaller woodland creatures include birch, oak, hawthorn, and hazel.

7. Choose a spot near the edge of the wood to place your house; make sure it's out of direct sunlight, sheltered from any rain, and not exposed to the wind (which might blow it over). A little way into the trees and off any path should do nicely, as we don't want to disturb any creatures once they're settled inside.

8. Look for ways to blend the house even more into its new surroundings. Cover it with dead leaves, more twigs, and even some soil to insulate against cold weather—just remember not to cover the air vents!

9. Leave fresh water outside, if you like.

10. Come back once a year to clean the house, but only if there are no creatures currently in residence!

IDENTIFY ANIMAL TRACKS

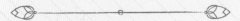

Sometimes, one of the first clues that you're in the presence of some-thing magical—or any animal at all—can be what you see around you. Many mammals leave easily identifiable tracks in the wood. Maybe you just missed a bear or deer leaving the area. There are four common groups: zigzaggers, waddlers, bounders, and hoppers.

- **ZIGZAGGERS** walk very carefully to save energy and leave a zigzag pattern that is easy to find. Zigzaggers include deer, moose, and foxes, among others.
- **WADDLERS** walk from side to side moving their whole body as they go. Waddlers include animals like bears, skunks, raccoons, and beavers.
- **BOUNDERS** move forward with a leaping motion that leaves two neat prints side by side, a gap, and then two more neat prints side by side. A common bounder in the woods would be otters.
- **HOPPERS** make a leapfrogging pattern, and include creatures like rabbits, chipmunks, and squirrels.

You can use the visual clues and the chart here to help you know just who's been walking in the woods near you.

1. Go for a walk in the woods, paying close attention to the forest floor.

   NOTE: Soft mud and soil, sand, or snow are all helpful ground condi-tions for capturing animal tracks, so a cold or muddy area may be an easy place to start.

2. Take a close look at any marks you see in the ground and try to identify the *track pattern*.

3. Have a look near any tracks you find to see if you can also spot other signs of an animal's presence such as droppings, bits of fur caught on brambles or twigs, well-worn paths not made by human feet, or nibbled nuts (squirrels split them in two with their teeth) and chewed-up pine cones. These other signs can help narrow down what type of animal made a certain set of prints.

4. Carry this book with you on your next woodland adventure and use the chart of tracks to help you more closely identify some of the most common animal tracks.

MOOSE DEER RACCOON POSSUM

BOAR COUGAR BEAR BEAVER

FOX WOLF SKUNK HEDGEHOG

CHIPMUNK RABBIT SQUIRREL OTTER

PACK AN ADVENTURE BAG

When you're going into the woods—whether you only plan to be there for a few hours or to spend the whole day—it never hurts to be prepared. Plans change, storms roll in unexpectedly, and sometimes, even when we don't mean to, we get turned around on our path. Below you'll find some suggestions of the best things to put in your backpack or other day bag the next time you're planning a hike or other adventure.

The Essentials

- **A GOOD BAG!** This could be a backpack or other sturdy bag; have an adult help you choose something that can stand up to wear and tear outdoors if you're unsure.
- **STAINLESS STEEL WATER BOTTLE.**
- **FOOD:** Protein bars or other snack bars, trail mix, and dried fruit are some ideas to keep your energy up for exploring.
- **WATERPROOF RAIN COVER:** You could even clip this onto the outside of your bag using a carabiner to save space.

- **JACKET OR OUTER LAYER:** Some parts of the wood are cooler than others, and it never hurts to be prepared.
- **BASIC FIRST AID SUPPLIES:** If you're unsure what should go into a basic first aid kit, ask an adult for some guidance.
- **HEADLAMP OR FLASHLIGHT:** In case it gets dark quicker than expected.

Other Suggestions

- **HAT:** For sun protection.
- **INSECT REPELLENT:** This won't keep you from seeing enchanted insects, but it will prevent those annoying mosquito bites.
- **SUNSCREEN.**
- **MOSQUITO NETTING:** For areas where insect repellent isn't enough protection.
- **HAND SANITIZER OR WET WIPES.**
- **SCOPE OR SMALL BINOCULARS:** For spotting animals from a safe distance.
- **BAG FOR LEAF COLLECTING:** If you'd like to make leaf prints at home.
- **SMALL JOURNAL:** To take notes on your adventures.

QUIZ

WHAT'S YOUR WOODLAND CREATURE PERSONALITY?

Ever wonder what kind of magical woodland animal you would be in another life? Perhaps you would splash and play in streams all day with the enchanted salmon, giving rides on your back to adventurous chipmunks, or maybe you would keep secrets and obscure facts stuffed in your shell like an enchanted turtle. Find out which group of magical creatures best matches your personality by answering the questions below.

Choose the responses that best fit for you and follow the prompts until you reach your first result. The result number tells you what your woodland creature personality would be.

1. How do you feel about flying?
    a. Love it!
    b. No way—give me a road trip any day.

If you chose b, skip to question 3!

2. When you're working on a group project for school, you are most often:
    a. The group leader—I'm good at seeing the big picture.
    YOU GOT RESULT #1!
    b. The one taking the most notes—I pay attention to detail.
    YOU GOT RESULT #2!

3. How do you feel about the water?
    a. I love it!
    b. It's all right.
    c. I can't stand it.

If you chose b or c, skip to question 5!

4. If a fairy appeared and told you that she could turn you into one of the merfolk, would you accept?
    a. Yes, I practically live in the water already.
    YOU GOT RESULT #3!
    b. No, I like being near the water, but I'd rather have fun on the beach.

5. Do you like being outdoors in the summer heat?
    a. I practically live out there!
    YOU GOT RESULT #4!
    b. It's not my favorite.

6. Which is your ideal pet?
    a. Something soft and snuggly, like a dog, cat, or rabbit.
    YOU GOT RESULT #5!
    b. Something with feathers or scales for me.
    YOU GOT RESULT #6!

RESULTS
Meet Your Magical Match

#1 BIRDS: You are able to spread your wings and rise above a situation to see the big picture; you're a natural leader and well suited to guiding others.

#2 ARTHROPODS: You pay attention to the details others miss or overlook; you have some natural artistic ability and aren't afraid to show off your unique style.

#3 FISH: You know there is wisdom and healing in the water. You're not afraid to live life at your own pace and appreciate the things that come your way.

#4 REPTILES: You know that warm weather and time spent in the sun cures all. You enjoy being active and are known among your friends for being a great secret keeper.

#5 MAMMALS: Family and friends are important to you; you thrive best when surrounded by the support of those you love, and in return, you would do anything for them.

#6 AMPHIBIANS: You are adaptable to a variety of situations and environments. You can fit in and find happiness anywhere and make the most of what you've been given.

QUIZ

WHAT'S YOUR HIDDEN MAGICAL POWER?

Answer the questions below to discover which type of magical ability you would have if you were a mysterious woodland creature. Choose the responses that best fit for you and follow the prompts until you reach your first result. The result number tells you what your magical power would be.

1. Do you belong to any sort of scout troop or volunteer group? Do you perhaps walk dogs at a local shelter or otherwise help out your community?

    a. Yes, I'm known for helping others.

    b. I like to help in my own ways when I can, but I don't volunteer often.

If you chose b, skip to question 5!

2. In your friend group, you are:

    a. The one who gives the best hugs.

       YOU GOT RESULT #1!

    b. The one who always has a plan when something goes wrong.

    c. The one who knows all the best gossip.

       YOU GOT RESULT #2!

    d. The one who knows exactly what's going on (like when next week's history test got moved to).

3. Are you good at solving the mystery in a book or show before the characters do?

 a. Yes, and they can be so predictable sometimes.
  YOU GOT RESULT #3!

 b. No, I enjoy them, but they keep me guessing.

 c. I'm not a fan of mysteries.

4. Surprising but good things happen to you . . .

 a. Often, like I have a secret lucky charm.
  YOU GOT RESULT #4!

 b. Sometimes, and they're always welcome.

5. Which of these would you rather spend time doing?

 a. Listening to old music, looking through old pictures, telling stories about good memories—or reading tarot cards, making vision boards, writing down life plans and goals in a journal, and looking to the future.
  YOU GOT RESULT #5!

 b. I prefer living in the moment!

6. When faced with a frustrating problem, you:

 a. Take a step back and try to look at it from a distance to see what you might have missed.
  YOU GOT RESULT #6!

 b. Figure out what you can change right now to take some control of the situation.
  YOU GOT RESULT #7!

RESULTS
About Your Magic

#1 HEALING: You have a natural understanding of how people and animals' bodies work and are able to use this knowledge to help mend injured paws and even get rid of annoying colds. Just being near you is enough to help heal certain sicknesses and minor injuries.

#2 COMMUNICATION: You don't need a guide to tell you what that skunk is saying or why that flower is drooping so low today— you can ask them yourself, because your magic involves communication or the ability to speak with plants and animals.

#3 DISCOVERY: Things don't stay lost or hidden around you for long; your magic gently tugs you toward whatever you're missing. You can spot hidden magical creatures as easily as you can find a lost notebook.

#4 LUCK: You're always having a good day, because there's luck within you. You are able to share this wonderful gift with others and help them have a better day, too.

#5 CLAIRVOYANCE (PERCEIVING): You know more than most, because your magic allows you to glance into the past or peer ahead into the future—both of which can teach us a lot about each other, and ourselves.

#6 FLIGHT: You can leave all your troubles far below you, because you're able to lift yourself up into the air and coast among the clouds anytime you please. There's magic in your wings, which leave showers of glitter as you rise into the air.

#7 CONTROLLING THE ELEMENTS: Don't like the dark clouds that are gathering? You can change that. Whether it's an ability to shift the direction of the wind, bring the rain, or push the clouds back to reveal sunbeams and moonbeams, your magic involves controlling the elements of nature.

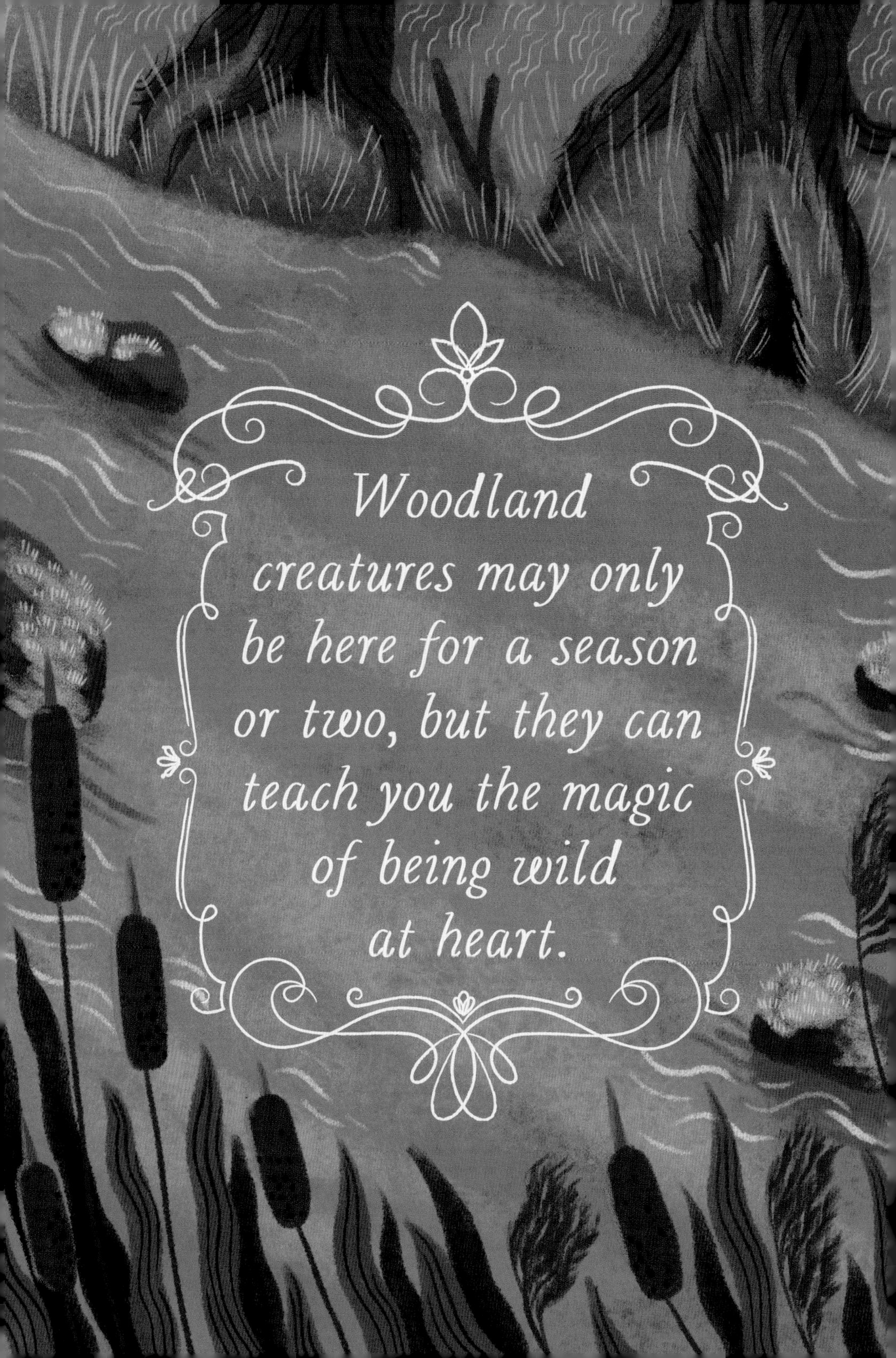
Woodland creatures may only be here for a season or two, but they can teach you the magic of being wild at heart.

Acknowledgments

When it's dark outside and a safe path through the twisty woods is hard to find, Allison Cohen and Katelyn Detweiler are always there to light the way! Other luminaries who kept the way forward clear as we shaped this book include Leah Gordon, Ashley Benning, and the whole team at Running Press, as well as Jill Grinberg Literary Management!

As always, many thanks to my family and friends for their wonderful support—especially to Dawn, who sees the magic in all creatures big and small just the way I do, and to my own pack of furry, feathered, and finned family. To my dad, who also loves creatures, and my mom, who got me my first dog even when she wasn't so sure about having that much hair in the house! As for my friends, like Erin, Sue, Sparks, Lenore, KT, Gwen, Vince, Josh, and Fox—I'd go camping with you all in the magical woods in a heartbeat; I might even scare off a bear for you, but let's hope we never have to find out!

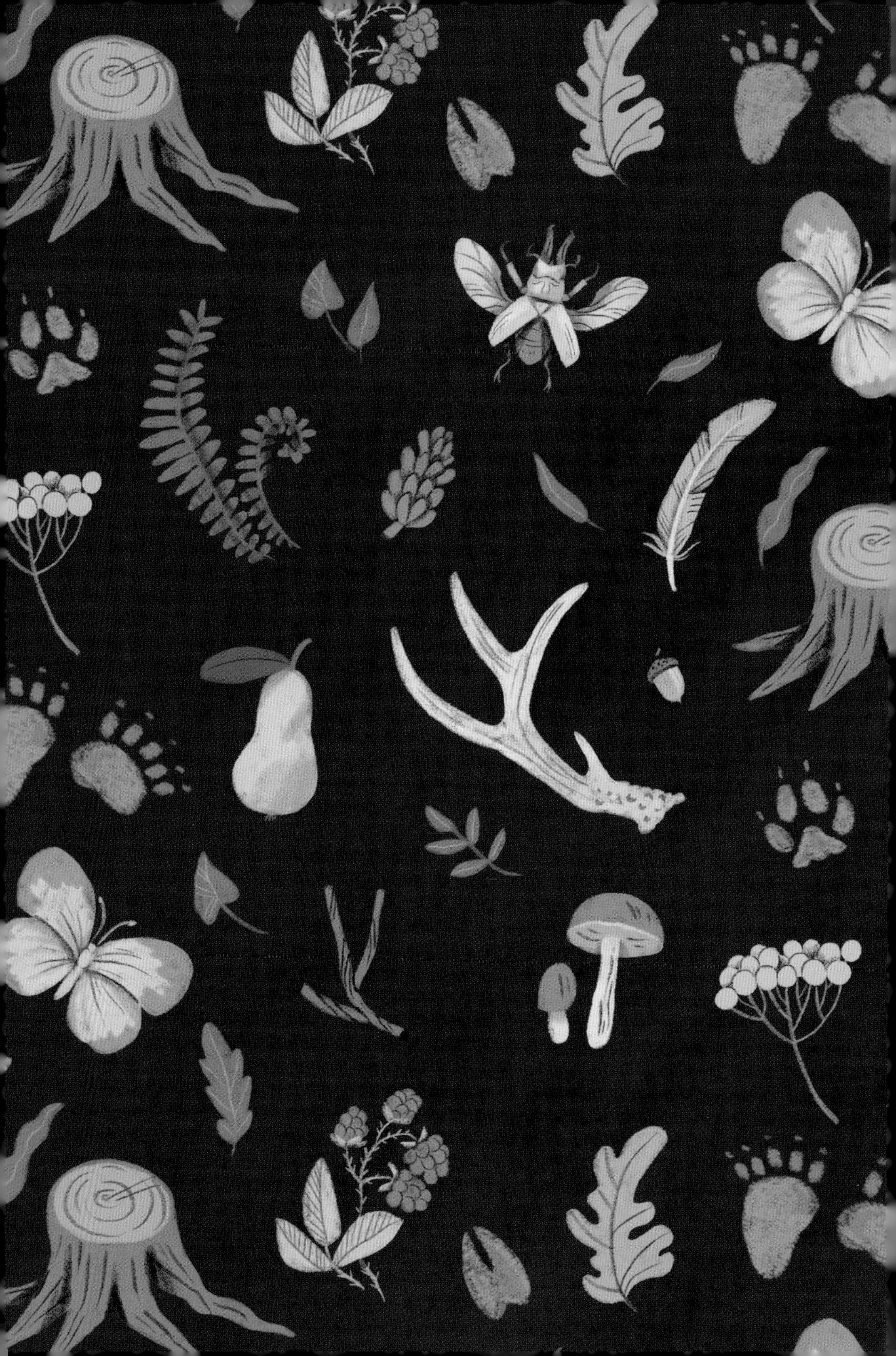

ABOUT THE AUTHOR

USA Today bestselling author **SARAH GLENN MARSH** has written several young adult novels and many picture books. Her Irish heritage has inspired a love of fairy folklore and fantastical storytelling from a young age. She lives with her husband, daughter, four dogs, several fish, and two birds in Richmond, Virginia. She enjoys spending time with all her pets when she isn't out roaming the woods in search of a little magic. Visit her online at www.sarahglennmarsh.com and let her know if you've ever spotted a magical woodland creature in the wild!

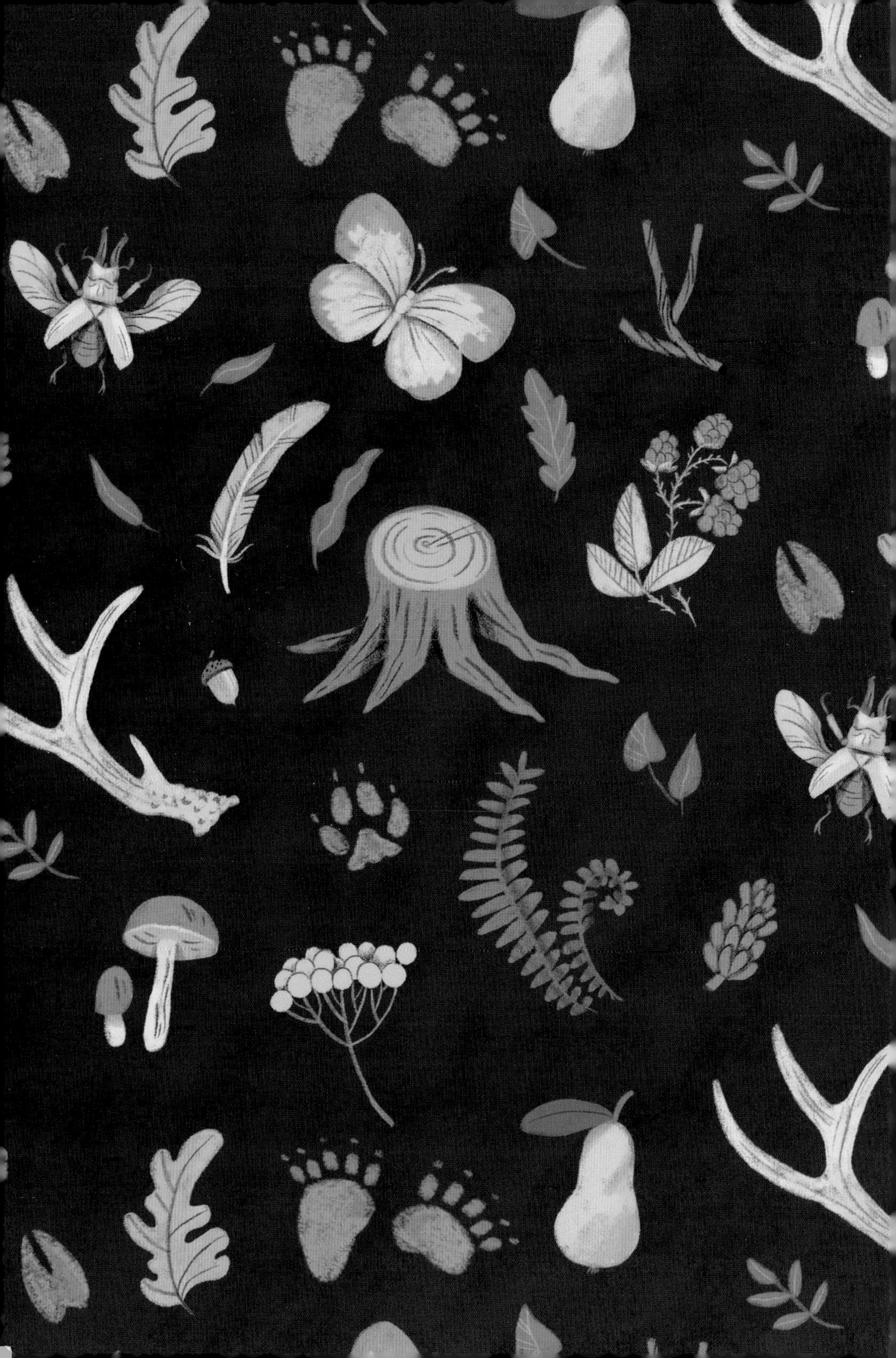

ABOUT THE ILLUSTRATOR

LILLA BÖLECZ is an artist and folklore lover who specializes in graphic art, book illustration, dollmaking, and pattern design. Her passion is to create peculiar, thought-provoking, mystical scenes and characters. Her work is mostly inspired by mysticism, legends, spiritual experiences, mythology, and literature. Lilla uses both digital and traditional media, including ink, gouache, clay, and acrylics. She is always looking for meaningful connections and to bring to life the unconventional and unique.

ALSO BY SARAH GLENN MARSH

HOW TO SPOT A FAIRY
A FIELD GUIDE TO SPRITES, SYLPHS, SPRIGGANS, AND MORE
SARAH GLENN MARSH
Illustrated by LILLA BÖLECZ

On Sale June 2025

HOW TO SPOT A MERMAID
A FIELD GUIDE TO MAGICAL SEA PEOPLE
SARAH GLENN MARSH
Illustrated by LILLA BÖLECZ

Your Birthstone Book
UNEARTH the SECRETS of YOUR BIRTHDAY GEM
Written by SARAH GLENN MARSH
Illustrated by HALLYE WEBB

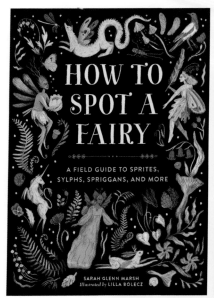

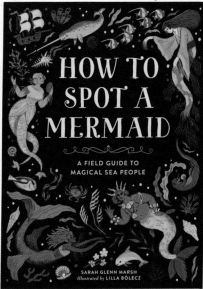

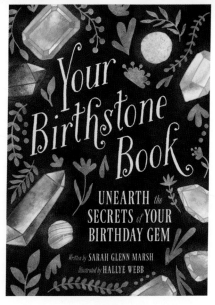

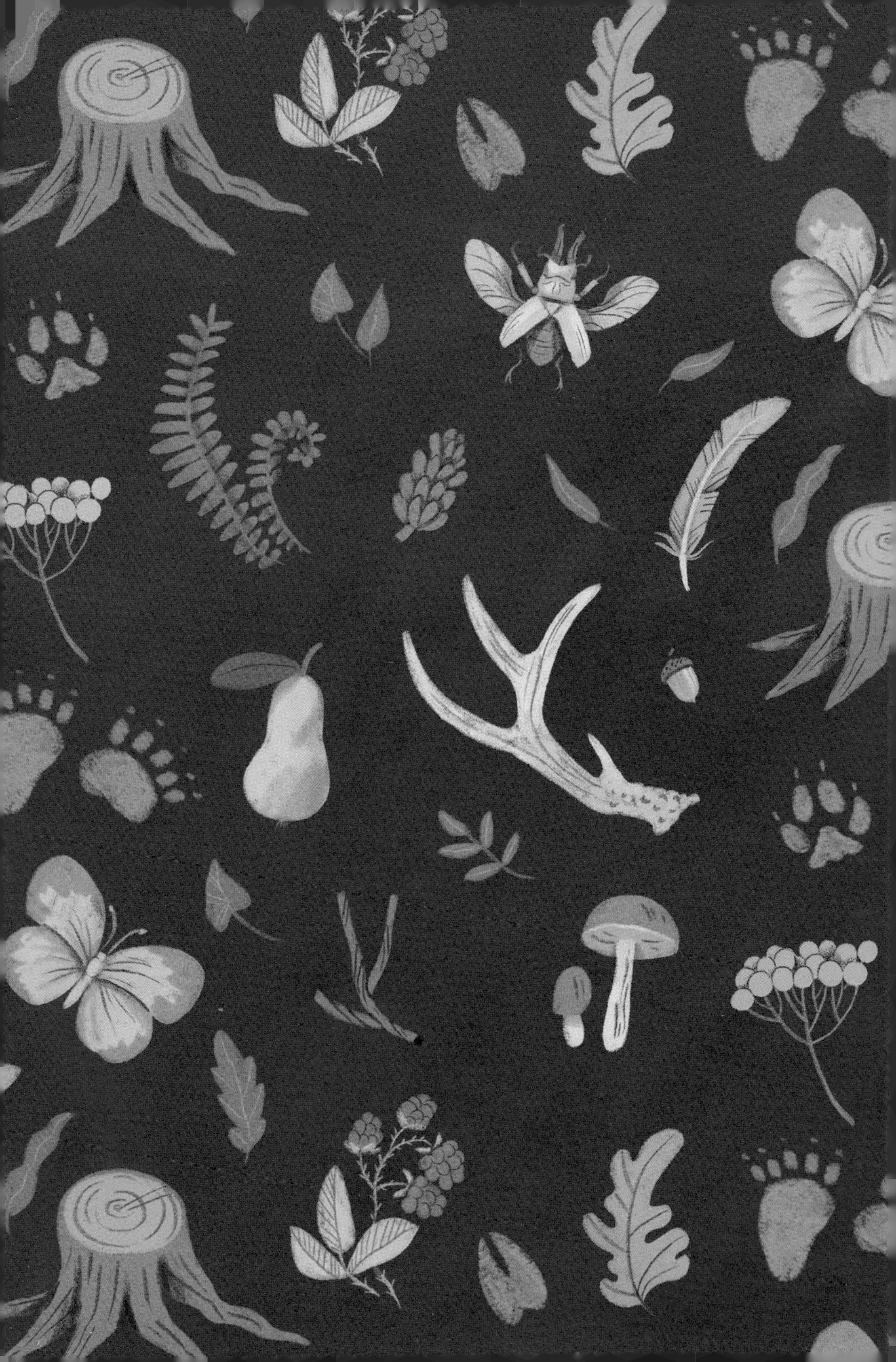